WE HAD
NO RULES

WE HAD NO RULES

STORIES

CORINNE MANNING

ARSENAL PULP PRESS
VANCOUVER

ARSENAL PULP PRESS
Suite 202 – 211 East Georgia St.
Vancouver, BC V6A 1Z6
Canada
arsenalpulp.com

Arsenal Pulp Press acknowledges the xʷməθkʷəy̓əm (Musqueam), Sḵwx̱wú7mesh (Squamish), and səlilwətaʔɬ (Tsleil-Waututh) Nations, custodians of the traditional, ancestral, and unceded territories where our office is located. We pay respect to their histories, traditions, and continuous living cultures and commit to accountability, respectful relations, and friendship.

This is a work of fiction. Any resemblance of characters to persons either living or deceased is purely coincidental.

The following stories have been previously published:
"The Boy on the Periphery of the World," *Southern Humanities Review*, Summer/Fall 2016; "Chewbacca & Clyde," *Vol. 1 Brooklyn*, Spring 2014; "Gay Tale," *StoryQuarterly*, Winter 2015; "Ninety Days," *Cascadia Magazine*, June 2019; "The Painting on Bedford Ave.," *Bellingham Review*, Fall 2016; "Professor M," *Moss*, Winter 2015 (mosslit.com); "Seeing in the Dark," *Wildness*, October 2017; "The Wallaby," *Joyland*, August 2017; "We Had No Rules," *Calyx*, Spring 2017

The poetry on page 167 is reprinted with permission from Alice Notley.

Front cover photograph: *Passing the Joint* by Amanda Kirkhuff
Cover and text design by Jazmin Welch
Edited by Shirarose Wilensky
Proofread by Alison Strobel

Printed and bound in Canada

Library and Archives Canada Cataloguing in Publication:
Title: We had no rules / Corinne Manning.
Names: Manning, Corinne, 1983– author.
Description: Short stories.
Identifiers: Canadiana (print) 20190217596 | Canadiana (ebook) 2019021760X | ISBN 9781551527994 (softcover) | ISBN 9781551528007 (HTML)
Classification: LCC PS3613.A356 W44 2020 | DDC 813/.6—dc23

For Ever

"It is this *queer* I run from. A pain that turns us to quiet surrender. No, surrender is too active a term. There *was* no fight. Resignation."

—CHERRÍE MORAGA,
"It Is You, My Sister, Who Must Be Protected," *Loving in the War Years*

CONTENTS

we had
no rules

My family had no rules. At least it felt that way for a time, because most of the rules were vague and unspoken: *don't lie, or steal, or hurt*. If I was mean to my sister, or my sister to me, we would apologize. We did the dishes together every night. We shared toys. When she read to me, I would thank her, and if I wanted her to read to me, she would, unless she had too much homework. Our parents' rules had to be enforced only after we broke them—after my sister broke them. By the time I was old enough to encounter the same dilemma, I already knew the edict, and through watching her, I knew what rules to follow. Which was why, at sixteen, I left home, just as my sister had, only I ran away because there was one rule I couldn't keep from breaking. If I knew anything about my parents it was where they stood, so why expect different results?

I was lucky, because when it was my turn, Stacy was twenty-four, set up in a rent-controlled apartment in Chelsea with only two roommates. She worked as a paralegal and attended classes at Hunter most nights. It was 1992, and I had a place to go.

Stacy was mad at first. She held my hand as we walked from the subway to her apartment, and I felt so much better now that my hand had a place to be. My hands get icy when I'm nervous. When I was little, Stacy used to rub them until they were warm again, and I wondered if she remembered this. I felt small and untethered as we walked down those streets, because I smelled perfume and trash and urine, saw posters of men kissing and women kissing, and because over the din of cars and voices I heard the roaring immensity of what I'd done.

"You gave them what they wanted," she said. She jerked my hand as we turned a corner.

I hadn't seen Stacy since she left, and she'd gone through a complete transformation. She traded running shoes for leather boots that went up to just over her knees and had huge heels. She towered over me by almost a foot. The bangles on her wrists clanked together, and her hair—which was shaved when I last saw her, a rule broken—was a gorgeous orange mess.

She had a unique kind of insight into what I was going through. "You made it easy for them. They want you to feel so ashamed that you leave. There's this way they pretend there're no rules, and they subtly suffocate you. That's what they did to me, only they posed it as a choice. If you wanted to do it differently, you would have given them the ultimatum, like: 'Either you accept me and we talk about this, or I'm getting the fuck out of here.'"

I pulled my hand out of her grip to adjust my shoulder bag, but I regretted it because afterwards her hand wasn't available anymore. She shoved it into the pocket of her neon-yellow hunting vest. I stayed close to her, taking as much comfort as I could from the rub of her arm against mine.

We paused at a traffic light and I could tell she wanted to bolt across, but she was trying to set a good example of how to cross the street. I leaned into her a little more.

"I'd rather be with you, though," I said. "I wanted to be with you."

It had been a long time since I'd seen her cry, and there was this way that tears just suddenly flooded around her lids—you wouldn't have known she was upset until this happened—like a mysterious dam had been opened. She grabbed my hand and rubbed her thumb briskly over my skin, then we ran together across the street.

When I arrived at the apartment, there was a closet made up like a room for me and her things were in bins just outside it. I didn't complain about having no window because she did some sweet things to the closet to make it feel like a room. She suspended a kind of mobile that her roommate Jill made out of spoon and fork handles. Her other roommate, who turned out to always be touring with some band, built a few shelves at the end of the closet so I could put my things up there. My main light was a paper lantern, and sometimes I felt like a caterpillar in a whimsical cocoon.

That first morning she took me to her favourite bakery and watched me eat two chocolate chip banana muffins, mine and hers.

"Look, I'm not going to totally police you, but you can't just bring home any girl, because you have to remember that this is also home to all of us, and if you and some girl decide to fuck—"

"Stacy!" I looked around to see if anyone had heard, but no one seemed bothered.

"If you decide to fuck, you have to be respectful. No shouting. I don't want to hear 'cause you're my baby sister, and Jill's room is right against that closet and you don't want to do that to her either. I've already told Jill and Toby this, but I'm going to say it to you, too—don't fuck my roommates. You can have sex with anyone as long as they aren't living with us at the time. You need to realize this—"

She leaned forward real close and I stopped chewing.

"You and I are partners now, and I worked hard to get this clean, safe apartment with these not-so-clean, stable people, and if you fuck it up, we are both out, and I know you don't know this yet, but sex is really fucking messy and what you get into will affect me too."

"I know about sex," I said.

Stacy smiled, then tried to hide it. "I'm pretty sure all you've done is hold hands under the covers at a sleepover and she let you kiss her neck while she pretended to be asleep."

I looked down and picked up some crumbs from the wax paper with my pointer and put them in my mouth.

"She was definitely awake," I said.

"I'm gonna take care of you," she said. "We're gonna figure out school, and I'll help you find a job. You won't go through what I went through. Okay?" She looked at me so seriously.

I nodded. I know that wasn't enough of an acknowledgment, but the fact that I even nodded is commendable, I think, at sixteen.

I didn't know, at this point, what she went through. I knew it was terrible, because early on she called my parents and left this message on the answering machine that made me tremble and cry because she was sobbing and saying she wanted to come home. She left a number for a pay phone, and when she answered, her voice sounded like mine, like a child's, and I begged my mom to get on the phone and listen. And my mom just kept saying, *You made your choice, you made your choice,* and I heard my sister on the other end screaming, *Please, please,* the word scraping away, digging for anything decent but striking rock after rock. I hid in the other room until, finally, one of them hung up.

After breakfast, I sat on the toilet lid and watched her get ready for work, just like I used to watch her get ready for school before she left home. She straightened her hair and brushed it out so that it lay smooth and thick around her shoulders. Her lipstick was modestly pink. I didn't breathe while she applied liquid eyeliner, for fear I'd somehow make her smudge it.

"I'll be home at two and I don't have to be in class until seven, so we can do whatever in between." She smiled at me in the mirror. I was wearing an outfit Mom had picked out for me—red cords and a pink turtleneck.

"Maybe we'll dress you in some different clothes. I'll call in some favours." She closed her eyeliner and dropped it into her purse. She pressed her cheek against mine in lieu of a kiss.

I was entranced: here I was, smelling her makeup again. When she closed the door, I felt a lonely kind of despair.

—

The phone rang—it rang and rang—and I followed the sound to the kitchen. This was my first view of Jill, who sat reading the paper in a tank top and boxers. She was very pale, her hair was dyed black and shaved underneath, and although that made her seem a little tougher than my sister, when she looked up at me, there was something flamboyantly soft about her.

"Don't answer it, mister," she said. "We screen."

A man's voice snapped on and I jumped.

"Hiii, this is Anthony. I like long messages." The machine beeped and there was the crackling sound of a phone returning to its cradle.

"Who was that?" I asked.

Jill took a slow sip from her mug. "Anthony. This is his apartment."

I looked over my shoulder. "Then where is he?"

"He's dead," she said, like it was very boring, very common. She turned the page.

"Oh, okay." I said. Then: "What from?"

She looked up at me. "The virus."

It took me a moment to put it together, but when I did I stated: "AIDS," very loudly, like I'd seen a spider, like the virus was on me. The panic hit me so hard that I would have started crying if I wasn't so afraid of Jill.

She looked at me with compassion, but her voice was still laced with boredom. "You can't catch it from living here. It's transmitted through sharing needles, or through blood or unprotected sex. Want some coffee?"

I didn't like coffee, but I said sure. She poured it into a cracked teacup with roses on it. She added tons of milk and sugar, then motioned to the seat across from her.

She wore something that smelled like Old Spice—I don't know whether it was aftershave or deodorant. It could have reminded me of my dad, but it didn't. I sipped from my little-kid coffee and examined the table. Much of the mail was addressed to Anthony. After a while, I spoke again.

"I'm a girl," I said.

She squinted at me.

14

"I just—you called me mister before, so I just wanted to make sure you knew."

She shut one eye, opened it, and then shut the other. "Of course. Bad habit. Last thing I want to do is fetishize my roommate's kid sister. 'Tis forbidden."

"Is today your day off?" I asked.

Her lipstick was so red that even though there was a mark on her coffee cup, there was still plenty on her lips, which she pursed as she folded the paper. "Sure is. If you were me, what would you do with today?"

I crossed and uncrossed my legs. I wasn't sure how to sit next to her. "I've only been to the city twice, and we just rode the Circle Line and had dinner at the Hard Rock Cafe."

Her face lit up. "Wanna ride the Staten Island Ferry and get a burger?"

"My sister's home at two."

"We'll be back way before then. Can I dress you up?"

—

She undressed in front of me, and when she took off her shirt I looked away. But I didn't when she was taking off her boxers, because she was talking to me at that point, and I thought she would have panties on underneath, so when I saw her bush— darker and thicker than mine, her furry thighs pinched around it—I pretended like I dropped something and bent down to look for it.

"What did you drop?" she asked.

"A bobby pin I was playing with."

"I didn't see anything fall," she said, and took a step towards me—still bottomless—to help me look for it, I thought, but she

15

put the clothes I was to borrow on the bed, then picked up a sequined dress from the floor and slipped it over her head.

"Found it!" I opened my hand, and then closed it quickly, but she didn't even look.

She was fiddling with something on her dress, so I stepped into the kitchen to change. From the doorway, I stared at her unmade bed while I pulled on the suit pants. I wondered how many people she had slept with. I put on the Depeche Mode T-shirt and tucked it in.

On cue, she stuck her head around the door frame. "Untucked," she said, and pulled the front and back out. "Your sister's like a redwood, but you and I are about the same height. Little shrubs."

She smiled, just inches from my face, and this was the first time I had to smile at someone who was standing this close to me, whose bush I'd seen, and who I didn't know very well. She helped me clip on the suspenders, but I wasn't sure where to let the straps rest—on the outside of my breasts, on the inside? Definitely not on top of them.

"I had a breast reduction," she said.

I looked at her chest.

"We threw a fundraiser."

I looked at my reflection in Jill's mirror. My sister and I had matching breasts, but on me they looked heavy and uncomfortable, which they were. The suspenders made them seem worse.

"Can I just let the suspenders hang down?" I asked.

"Absolutely." Then she pulled on a fur coat splattered with red paint. She told me she found it in the trash like that.

Once we were outside, she slipped her hand in mine. "Is this okay?" she asked.

I nodded.

"It's just that our outfits look so much better this way."

That afternoon, before she went to class, my sister and I ate pork roll and cheese sandwiches and planned my haircut. I didn't tell her much about my day with Jill—there wasn't much to tell, except for the way people looked at us, and how sometimes I wanted to drop Jill's hand, but she wouldn't let me. I didn't mention that I knew about Anthony, but when we were making our food in the kitchen, I didn't answer the phone when it rang and she said nothing about the message on the answering machine. I told Stacy that I liked the way Jill dressed me, so she added to my wardrobe—an ex's old combat boots and some more band T-shirts, most of which I hadn't heard of. She popped one of the records on while we got ready to do my hair. I heard my parents' voices screaming in the direction of her room: *Don't play music that loud!* I winced.

"She sounds angry," I shouted.

My sister laughed. "She is angry. You're not angry?"

I shook my head, and she replaced the album with one by another female musician, who sang haltingly over an acoustic guitar but still sounded urgent.

"I like this a lot better," I said.

"Well, Ani's pretty angry, too." Stacy pointed to a picture of her, taped in one corner of the mirror. She had a very pretty shaved skull.

My hair was cut as short as my parents would allow—a rule set in place after my sister—and I kept it pinned back with barrettes. Stacy pulled at a few of the longer pieces, then stepped back. She reached for something in her bag, and I thought it was going to be a pair of scissors, or a picture, but it was a pamphlet. She handed it to me, and I saw that it was for a youth program that

17

promised services I didn't totally understand, like job placement and training. It was filled with pictures of kids—a bouquet of races—who looked really happy but poor. With some of them I couldn't tell their gender, and I wondered if any of them had the virus.

"This says it's for at-risk youth," I said.

"That's you. That's who you are now."

I looked in the mirror, and I didn't know if I felt like one, and I wondered if I looked like one. A few of the kids in the picture who looked like girls had shaved heads.

I could hear Jill flipping through some videotapes in the living room. I wanted to get her opinion on my hair—maybe on the youth program, too—but she was staying away while Stacy was around. I wondered if she felt as seriously protective of the apartment as my sister did.

"I kind of want you to shave it," I said.

Stacy rubbed her hands over my head and nodded. "Rite of passage."

"But that seems kind of boring, and your head had a funny shape when it was shaved."

We both stared at me for a moment.

Then my sister's eyes opened wide, almost like she was laughing at a joke. "How about I try something and if you hate it, we'll just shave the rest of it off?"

When we came out of the room, it was just about time for Stacy to leave for school. Jill was sitting on the futon in a faded T-shirt and boxers, watching some Woody Allen movie, and when she saw me she nodded with deep approval.

"You two are so related."

The sides of my head were shaved and the very top was a little longer and teased in all directions, like in the Cure poster on Stacy's wall. I would have stared at my face and thought I looked like a chubby Frankenstein's monster, but Stacy and Jill kept saying how adorable I looked. I imagined how it might feel to have no breasts and this hair.

After Stacy left, I wanted to be present in the world with my haircut. I sat next to Jill and helped myself to a handful of her popcorn, which she didn't acknowledge, so I ate some more. I was bored: Woody was complaining and it was autumn in New York.

Jill's eyes started to close and her head bobbed once, then twice. I asked: "Do you have a significant other?"

She perked up and turned towards me. She closed one eye and then the other, and I felt like I knew something about her.

"You can say 'girlfriend' or 'dates,' or ask if I'm seeing anyone," she said.

"What do you mean 'dates'?"

"Some people have more than one."

"Okay, do you have dates?"

"Of course. Who doesn't? Oh wait, your sister." She moved the popcorn and settled more deeply into the futon, which meant, technically, that she moved closer to me.

"I don't think I do, either," I said. She didn't move, didn't react, so I kept going. "There was this girl I really liked, and I think she's gay too, but I don't know."

Jill leaned in close to me. Corn and butter accented her Old Spice smell. She snaked her arm around my shoulder and I didn't know what to do. I remembered what my sister had said. I kept my body stiff.

"Is this okay?" she asked.

I nodded.

She moved closer. "We both know your sister's rule."

I nodded again.

19

She pressed her lips to my ear and I thought I was going to throw up—I had no other sense of what that kind of urgency could mean. "Your first kiss should be with someone who isn't going to pretend that kiss isn't happening." Her lips on my ear made strange shapes out of the words.

I turned my head towards her. My haircut felt suddenly like just a haircut, and if she thought she was kissing a chubby baby Frankenstein's monster look-alike, she didn't show it. She pressed her lips onto my lips and my right hip twitched, and she laughed then kissed me again, and though it was strange to feel the metallic taste of another person's saliva, someone else's tongue, it was like I had always been kissing and could spend the rest of my life kissing. I didn't think of myself as foolish when I let the back of my hand rest on her stomach, but when she put her hand on my breast, I wasn't really sure if I liked it. I didn't say anything. I had no sense then that there could be some things I didn't have to like, that I could say no to.

She pulled away and sat a little farther from me on the futon. She folded her hands, and I wouldn't have been surprised if we started praying. I touched my hands together, too.

"I want to do something for you, but you have to understand that it's purely instructional, and that I'm not taking on any more dates, so you can't get jealous that you're not one of them. Jealousy just can't exist for you anymore, okay?"

I nodded. I was trying really hard to listen, but I just wanted her to kiss me again.

"This is purely instructional," she repeated, as she pulled off her boxers.

She shifted and I smelled her, and I felt embarrassed, mostly for myself. She spread her legs and took my hand, and it felt so different from when she held it on the Staten Island Ferry.

"I want to show you the G-spot. This is something I do for people. So I'll give you a latex glove and your finger will go inside me. Is that okay?"

I considered it. I didn't know what the appropriate reaction was for someone with a haircut like mine.

"Okay," I said, and I meant it. I felt a deep guilt already, like my sister knew what was happening. And I didn't want to go through what my sister had—I didn't want to ever say please the way she had—and as Jill brought my finger inside her and I watched it disappear with a gulp, I felt the certainty that someday I would say please like that, but I hoped it would be under much different circumstances.

"Okay, so press up." She winced. "No, with just the pad of your finger." She relaxed a bit. "Okay, so it should feel, like, marshmallowy, right?"

I nodded. "Is this sex?" I asked.

"No. Now palpate for a second. You should also feel something more like just behind the front teeth. Like ridges."

She made a little sound. I pressed my tongue behind my teeth and tried to compare it to what I could feel through my gloved finger, but there was no comparison. Her eyes were very distant, as if she were grading me based on an internal rubric. Beads of sweat bubbled up on her nose, little crystal domes. Should I ask if I could kiss her nose? Did I have any agency? I only moved as instructed.

"That's totally it." She smiled at me. "To me, it feels good and a little like I gotta pee."

She took my hand out of her, and I felt instantly cold. She pulled on her boxers. I held my damp gloved finger outstretched because I didn't know what to do with it. Onscreen, Woody had just broken a teenager's heart.

21

"How will I know if it's sex?"

She pulled the glove off and kissed my palm. "You'll just know." She turned off the movie and stretched her arms over her head. "I need to go to bed. I got a shoot in the morning and an action in the evening."

I didn't know what either of those meant, and I didn't want to be alone yet with this hand, so I just chose the first one.

"Shoot, like needles?" I asked.

"No, like movies."

"An actress," I said.

"Sort of but more kinda like porn."

"Oh, okay, cool," I said.

She pinched my cheek. "A friend of ours makes it. It's fun." She closed one eye—I waited—but not the other one. She stood, so I stood. "You can ask your sister more about it."

She opened the door to my closet, and I climbed in like I was a pet. I didn't tell her that I hadn't brushed my teeth yet, that it was eight p.m. and I wasn't tired. I switched on the light before she shut the door. Through the wall, I listened to the sound of her bed creak as it took her in.

—

The phrase *You can ask your sister more about it* tormented me all night. I couldn't wait very long in the morning. It was a great act of will that I let Stacy go to the bathroom, take a bite of her toast, drink her coffee. I stared and stared at her, and she looked up at me a few times before finally closing her textbook.

"You're creeping me out."

"Does Jill do court work too?"

"No, kind of odd jobs."

"Like what?" I asked. I tried to look as nonchalant as I had last night when my finger was inside Jill.

"Studio assistant work, medical studies." She paused for a moment, made a decision. "Sex work," she added.

"Oh, okay, cool," I said. "So like porn?"

"Including porn. A range of things." She glanced down at the cover of her book and ran her fingers down the front as if to open it but set it aside instead.

"I did that for a while," she said.

I flinched and covered my face.

"You're thinking of channel sixty-eight, all scrambled?"

I kept my face covered. I wasn't going to say anything about the moans, the flash of a boob, a mouth pulsing on a rod.

"It wasn't quite like that—though there's a place for what happens on channel sixty-eight. If it was photos, sometimes I'd have to stay still with my back arched for, like, half an hour, but the people I worked with were positive and respectful."

I heard her mouth bite into toast. I still didn't want to expose my face. I felt like I didn't want to know all of this—that a G-spot existed, or what a breast reduction was. I didn't want my haircut or a youth program. I wanted to be home, with my barrettes and my sleepovers and my TV. And my parents.

"You remember when I called home?" she asked.

I pulled my hands away from my face. She looked stiff and tense, like she wanted out of this conversation too, but neither of us could stop it.

"It was bad. I didn't know what was going to happen. Literally, when I got off the phone, it was like a miracle—a woman I had met at a shelter came by and told me about this gig she had with this photographer, Anthony. Turns out he was looking for 'young radical women' and she got me a shoot. That's where I

23

made friends who connected me to the community. Someone even helped me figure out GED stuff. When Anthony got diagnosed, he didn't want his landlord or anyone in the building to know—landlord's son was sniffing around, tripling the rent on apartments. And he wanted to control something. He went and stayed with his boyfriend, told the landlord I was his sister, that he'd be working abroad for a while, and the three of us moved in."

She took my cold hands and rubbed them in hers.

"It's not like it's something you have to do, unless, of course, you decide that's something you want. You can choose what you want to be ashamed of. But you don't *need* to be ashamed of me."

Her hands, I noticed, were cold too.

"This is totally different from home," she continued. "And if you wanted to try to go back and just wait it out until you're eighteen, I'd get it. Most people manage that way. But I promise, if you stay, I'll take care of you. Things will feel different, but that's good. Whatever you're afraid I went through when I first ran away you're going through too, but in the gentlest way possible."

We sat there, our icy hands clutched together. Outside, I heard the honking of horns, and I felt the rolling jitter of a jackhammer shaking me out on the inside.

"If I stay, we'll to have to move." I pressed her hands to my forehead. "I broke the rules, I think."

I gulped and snorted, and she kept her hands clenched on mine and brought them down to look at them. I don't know what she saw there, what she was figuring out, how my hand could have possibly looked different from before last night, but she snapped her eyes to mine. We held our eyes there, and in that pause I wanted her to see what happened. I wanted her to tell me that it wasn't sex. But instead, she waited, and I saw the worry spreading across her face, so finally I spoke.

24

"Jill wanted me to have a good first kiss, so she kissed me."

The tension on her face eased and her shoulders shifted. She stifled a smile, then put my hands down.

"That's—you know—that happens. Did you like it?" There was a quavering in her eyes, and I knew what she wanted my answer to be, and I wanted my answer to be the same as hers.

"I liked it a lot," I said. "But it doesn't need to happen again."

"I'm glad it was nice. We don't have to move, but yeah, let's not have that happen again."

She picked up our dishes and I walked with her to the sink. We stood beside each other the way our mom taught us before Stacy left: her hands in the soapy water, mine drying what she handed me. I dried dishes until every drop of water was gone, *because you don't put away wet plates*. The cabinet was up high, and I stood on my tiptoes and wondered whether I could slide the dishes in without breaking them. I turned to get a chair—*because no one is gonna help you; you gotta help yourself*—but Stacy took the plate out of my hand, soap suds in a bracelet around her wrist as she reached for the cabinet above my head.

gay tale

Oh, fuck it. I'm writing lesbian fiction. I know I'd do better to write gay fiction, or in some academic circles, queer fiction. How many people, I wonder, have stopped reading already? A lot of lesbians are scary, and weird. I don't even like the word.

One time, before I was considered a lesbian, my boyfriend and I were getting ice cream in our small Southern college town. It was one of those incredibly warm February days when it's unclear what season it might ever be. Our cones were high and melting quickly, so we licked away fervently as we strolled to the water. A French bulldog approached us with balls so large it seemed like it would be anatomically difficult for him to walk uphill, but he was doing it, and snorting and panting.

"Oh, hell-oooo," Ron crooned. He bent down and the dog wagged his tail, sending his balls back and forth like magical pendulums.

"Hi, friend, hi," I said, scratching just above the dog's butt. The dog licked at the air, his claws clacking against the ground as he spun in slow circles to appreciate both of us.

"That ice cream you got looks good," the owner said, stepping forward.

Now that I'm considered a lesbian, I know it's incorrect to assume you know someone's pronoun, but I don't know if you're ready for me to use the singular they. At this point in the story, I'm still concerned about what you are ready for. She wore long khaki shorts that went to just below the knee—I was crouched down, so I stared at what was visible of her shins. She had a sturdy, stocky body—a powerful man's shape—and breasts that inflated her black polo. Her pale skin had seen so much sun that it looked ready to slough off. She had a head like a bean, with a very small and handsome face, with brown eyes as deep and round as her dog's.

"This is a great dog you got here," Ron said.

"His name's Jasper. I'm Sam," she said, looking at me.

I pictured her naked, saw the muscled legs, hips and back, the sagging breasts, and—I couldn't help it—giant balls, like Jasper. It was one of the most beautiful images I'd ever held in my brain. I was certain that she could see it, too. How could she look like that and not be psychic?

"I've got two cats and another dog that doesn't like to go out much 'cause he's old. I got a parakeet that screams all day long. I had two parakeets, but one of the cats ate one. I didn't cry because I was happy that Susie got to do what she's supposed to."

I turned away, politely, to get my tongue around the cone more where it was starting to drip, and also to signal that it was time to be moving on. It seemed like there might be something wrong with Sam. She stared at me harder, and I realized that the whole time she'd been rambling she'd only been looking at me.

"That ice cream sure looks good. I'd get chocolate ice cream, and then I'd get cherry, but I don't think I'd get it in a cone because my hands always got this grease on them from work, you know. I got two jobs and I own my own house and I got a riding mower."

She's trying to turn me into a lesbian, I thought. I could feel her in my brain, working something the way she might work an engine. I heard a sputtering in some wiring. I touched Ron's back, underneath his T-shirt.

"Well, we'll be seeing you," he said, and we continued on to the water. I felt her watching us.

"What a strange person," Ron said. "She must be so lonely here. I wonder if she gets to date much."

"Probably why she has all those animals," I said.

I imagined her undressing me, how excited she'd be, how she'd keep talking even as I was sitting in front of her naked. It wasn't that I wanted to be with her, but I felt moved that I could be wanted that way. Ron and I looked out at the water, and as I sat there, in my brain, naked in front of Sam, I felt so feminine. I moved my shoulders the way I imagined Marilyn Monroe might move hers, and I lifted my chest and exposed my neck. I am so hot, I thought. Never before had I considered making love to myself. It seemed like it must be fantastic.

"What are you doing?" Ron asked. His face had a laughing shape, and I felt something snap off in me quickly. I felt cold. "You were moving your shoulders in this funny way. I loved it."

29

He leaned over and kissed me, and even though I often felt shy in public, I kissed him back this time, thinking of her seeing us, and then picturing myself, and I felt whatever had snapped off a moment ago return.

—

On our first date, Ron looked at me from his side of the table and said, with great conviction, "I'm into guys."

"Oh," I said, slightly disappointed and confused, not because he liked boys but because he said it in a way that suggested he only liked boys.

"Are you into girls?" he asked me.

"Maybe. I don't know."

After dinner, he brought me into an alley and pressed me against a building. We quickly found ourselves in a habit of having sex in public places: against a highway overpass, on the toilet seat of a gas station restroom, midday in a park with a father and son looking out from the bleachers. The man stood watching us, not in an interested way but more to let us know he'd seen. What I felt, specifically, as I sat up and looked at him, was that he wanted to make sure that I, not Ron, was the one who knew he saw.

After meeting Sam and her dog, I imagined my breast in her mouth as Ron and I made love. I ached for this scenario to come true, to have him on top of me and to have her, or some other woman, there, doing that.

"Can you tell me about the time you gave that queen a blow job?" I asked afterwards, curled against him.

He yawned and stretched his long thin body fully; his hands pressed against the wall and his feet hung off the bed. "I was helping her dress between sets. I lifted up her skirt. She pushed me away."

"And you liked it?" I asked. This was the question I always asked, as if I could glean more information from the retelling than I already had.

"You know, thinking back on it now, I don't know how much I did. I felt really excited that I was doing it, but I felt really scared afterwards that I would get sick or something."

"What do you mean, 'thinking back on it now'?" I asked.

He rolled to face me and pulled my body against his. "I think it was a phase or something. The longer I'm with you, the less I think I'm actually gay. Do you ever just like the idea of something? I think I really like the idea of gay men, but I don't think I'd want to be in a relationship with a guy. I'd miss how soft girls are." He jostled my breasts in his hands like they were some other thing. "I'd miss these ladies," he said, and then put one in his mouth.

When Ron left me, not too long after that night, I cried. It was like some lever got pulled, and I wondered if the lesbian and her dog hadn't rewired something in him, too. He realized that he didn't want to marry me, and he couldn't get the thought out of his head. He'd once told me that he didn't believe in marriage. "I'm not going to get married until it's legal for all people to get married," he'd said. I was suddenly a waste of time, like I was this dead-end retail job he'd been working for seven years.

Right before he got into the moving truck, his body jolted with sobs, and I held him and told him he was going to be okay and "Go get 'em," though I didn't know who "'em" were. I was grateful he was crying and I wasn't.

That night, I walked along the water and saw Sam-the-Lesbian sitting next to a woman who was thinner and prettier than me

31

but in a way that was hard to trust, that suggested she had been a slut in high school, a magnet for all bad things. Sam didn't notice me as I walked by, even though I slowed down, hoping they'd see me as one of them. The dog, Jasper, sniffed and lifted his head. He stood and I saw his testicles were gone. I covered my mouth and my body convulsed in preparation for a sob, and then it passed.

—

I started spending my evenings at the Sphinx, the one gay bar in town, and paced the floors drinking cup after cup of water. What I gathered was that if I kept moving the whole time, no one would see me—the opposite strategy of avoiding a T. Rex. One floor of the club was decorated like a jungle, another like a desert, and I would run my hands through the ferns and along murals of sand dunes. On the top floor was a sauna that reeked of genital varieties, and at least once a night I'd pass through, feeling my T-shirt stick to my back and watching the sweating doors.

Then one night, after making my first round, I went to the cooler to refill my water and the cup slipped from my hand and fell to the floor in an explosion of liquid. I bent to pick it up, and paused for a second to look at the coloured glass that was embedded in the floor, when I saw the beginning of ankles and then shins and then knees. I looked up and up, at this very thin person with a crisp ironed dress shirt and a shaved head.

"I'm Rachel," she said. I just looked at her and squeezed the plastic cup and imagined the cracking sound I would have heard if the music wasn't so loud.

"Are you lost?" she asked.

"What?"

"Are you lost?"

One of my contact lenses went dry and stabbed my eye. I blinked rapidly a few times, watching her all the while.

"I've been telling my friends I think that girl took a wrong turn and can't figure out how to get out of this place."

"I'm not sure if I want you in this story," I said. "Because once you're here, they're going to expect me to go home with you."

"Isn't that how that goes? Do you want to disappoint them?"

"But they'll stop reading." I accepted the hand she offered and stood, and felt a little disappointed that I was a few inches taller than her.

"All the queers are reading, worried that you're going to end the story getting back with a man. My friends told me not to come over and talk to you because you're probably bi, but I have nothing against that."

Rachel's features were so delicate, like she was made out of unfired clay. I reached out and touched the tip of her nose with my finger, surprised that it was warm and didn't crumble off and fall to the floor.

"Well?" she asked. "I can hear my friends—chirp-chirp-chirp—in my ear."

"I didn't realize they'd keep reading if I ended up with a guy again."

"A return to the world of men. But even that's risky. You don't seem straight enough to pull it off."

"I don't know what you should tell your friends," I said. I felt like one of those sexy tall women next to her, and I rested my elbow on her shoulder and looked down at her face. Her eyes were so light I couldn't tell what colour they were. She put her arm around my waist.

33

"I don't think you want my friends in this story, so let's not go over there. I don't think you want a dance scene, do you? Unless you want to write that I moved my body 'wildly like a rag doll' or that you 'felt the litheness of your own.'"

"I don't really like to dance," I said.

"You like to walk, though." She smiled a very pleased smile, then asked, "Would you take a walk with me outside? I know this place is endlessly fascinating, but I think we might see more variety if we head towards the water."

It wasn't a cold night, but I shivered from the drop in temperature and felt more exposed with the sudden absence of sound and pounding bass. Rachel looked even tinier outside. She started to put her arm around my waist again, but I stepped away. A group of boys in baseball hats were making their way dizzily to a car.

"We may be in a Southern town, but this is the Common Era," she said, and offered me her arm.

"I'm shy with public stuff," I said.

She rolled her eyes and started walking, and I could hear what she was saying in her brain: *My friends were right.* So I hurried alongside her and grabbed her hand. We both stopped walking for a moment. The space between us was a packed mass of wires, and I felt them weaving in and out of us. I opened and closed my free hand over the plastic cup and let the cracking sound serenade whatever was happening.

"Homos!" a voice called from the group of boys, and Rachel and I both doubled over laughing, only her laughter was real. I took the moment to slip my hand out of hers.

"It's true," she called out to them. "You found two!"

We kept walking towards the water, only now the wires, not our bodies, were holding us together. I looked at the cup in my hand and imagined I could turn myself into water and pour into it, away from Rachel, out of everyone's sight.

"You okay?" she asked. "Was that your first one?"

I was afraid I might cry if I said yes. My throat felt like cheap thread was twined around it. "That really happened," I said. I paused to toss the cup in the trash.

A couple walked by, wrapped around each other. The girl was practically leaning all of her weight on the guy, and it appeared that at some point in the night she had misplaced her shoes. They looked us over, and then looked politely away.

"They're thinking of us having sex," I said.

"Who?"

"They're trying to picture it. I saw her look at my jaw, and I could tell she was thinking something like: *That's been in a cunt.*"

"The readers, or those people?"

"Now the readers are," I said.

"They aren't. They can't picture you."

We stepped onto the boardwalk and climbed down onto one of the docks. A famous TV show used to film here, and I pictured the episode where the girl next door sat next to her childhood best friend, whom she now loved. I pulled my knees to my chest like she did.

"You stop thinking things like that after a while," Rachel said. "Once you feel normal to yourself again, you forget that other people don't see it that way. Sort of forget. It doesn't become about sex anymore, I guess is what I'm trying to say."

"What does it become about?"

Rachel gave a half shrug that was vaguely feminine and vaguely masculine. In a different outfit it would have seemed like a Marilyn Monroe move, but I was not in the mood to try it out.

35

"Stupidity, I think. Like annoyance over the presence of stupidity. You get to see more, which is a different kind of pain. But good, I think."

I watched a rowboat cut through the darkness. Someone held a flashlight and shone it on us, then quickly pulled it away. There were other docks for them to pull in at.

"The queers want you to be wary of me," I said.

"I know. I'm supposed to be afraid of getting involved with you because you're going to freak out at some point and break up with me. But right now, I'm finding your lack of history and baggage refreshing. I'm so glad that you don't have a coming out story yet, that you don't have some kind of weird ongoing situation with your family."

"You have those things?" I asked.

"Let's pretend we're like that couple we passed on the road. Let's not learn much about each other until after we've spent a month fucking, and let's not admit we're in love until about three months in, and let's not even consider moving in together."

Rachel leaned over and took off her boots and then her socks. She stood and stripped down to her underwear and T-shirt. Small breasts. No testicles. She dove into the water and I held tight to the dock that swayed in her wake.

I eased my body into the water and paddled out after her. She swam in long sure strokes, sometimes disappearing under water, and then re-emerging many feet away like a smooth-skinned sea creature. I panted in my doggy paddle, and she took pity on me and floated on her back, waiting. A larger boat was docked a bit away, but I could hear their music and the rumble of men's voices. I considered veering off and swimming towards that boat, but I couldn't imagine letting their voices get louder and gain definition.

36

I doubted I would return to the world of men, but I knew I would end this story before the sex scene. My arms were exhausted. I coughed, and paused. Rachel took one large stroke to meet me.

Professor M

The dog wasn't mine anymore. It belonged to her, and so did the house, and the sixties-style turquoise bookshelf that we purchased together, the pots and pans, the soap dish in the bathroom. They were her idea.

"Intellectual property," she shouted at me during a fight in which we were both sobbing.

"That's for articles and screenplays, not Boris." I pressed my face into the dog's neck and gave a deep moan that came from somewhere untouched, like the socket of my hip. It startled all of us. Boris turned and licked at my face. "I can't be without this dog."

"Well, I don't know what to do." Julia bit her lip. She watched me from across the room and tore at this one sad piece of her hair that took the brunt of all her stress. Back when we weren't in the process of breaking up I would have pulled her hand away. Sometimes I would kiss it. But now it made an awful snapping sound, and I could picture the day when, without my intervention, that patch of hair would wilt and crumple to the floor, leaving a quarter-sized bald spot. I tugged between the satisfaction of that image and the dwindling part of me that wanted only sweet, good things for her.

"We would have to see each other pretty regularly, and I just don't think I could handle that after what you've done," she said.

These words worked like a spell. I kissed Boris's neck and smelled pine and shit and some chemical from the dog's shampoo. I rubbed between her eyes, and then stood with my duffle bag.

"I'll come by next weekend to pick up my books."

When Boris was a puppy, she sat in my lap and I held her, totally enamoured by her softness, her buttery bones and joints, how she seemed ready to spill out into my hands.

"This is why people have babies," I'd said to Julia. "When they're soft like this, I bet you can really feel their souls."

Of course, I can't imagine what it would feel like to hold a human soul in my hands, but holding Boris, her soul available and pliable like paraffin, was one of the greatest things I'd ever done. I felt like I was connected to her soul in this very pure way, so even after she became muscled and fully formed, with the proud broad chest of a bulldog, I could stare into her eyes and still feel the—how else can I say it?—availability of her spirit.

—

There is a trauma to making a mistake and not being forgiven. To being held so accountable that your life is stripped from you. That act itself is unforgivable. Though I know I should feel guilty, and I do, though I know I caused Julia pain, nothing I did warrants her reaction.

I'm embarrassed that I could live out such a predictable storyline. As a professor of queer theory, or as my university prefers, women and gender studies, I feel it is important to demonstrate to my students other modes of possibility and living. My young queer students always fall in love with me. They love my well-fitting slacks, my bow ties. They swoon when I ask them to just call me Professor, in lieu of gender pronouns. I've watched them follow the line of my waist to my jaw as I speak. While they work in small groups I can feel their eyes on me as I sit, stoic, fucking their essays. I'm a scholar who prefers to be a teacher, and it doesn't matter that most of my students are bad lays. I get a queer, aching joy from their misfired connections, their wimpy arguments, my red pen circling a clause like a tongue.

"I want you to stun me," I told this group at the beginning of the semester. "Give me a reason to hold my pen up but not actually put it down."

I watched them all scribble this into their notebooks, except for one student, Taylor, who watched me as acutely as I liked to watch them. In my first few years of teaching, this would have really thrown me off. I would have looked down, messed with my papers, glanced at the clock, coughed. Now, I'm a professional. They only need to share their names once at the beginning of the first class and I already have them memorized.

"Is there a problem, Taylor? Something you want to question?"

"I'm good. Just watching."

"It might serve you to write some of this information down."

"Don't need to. It's in the syllabus."

The other students popped their heads up at me. This was the opportunity to get my class size down. Taylor had served me for a spike.

"If you are someone who does very well in all your other classes, I guarantee you'll do poorly in this class."

Taylor revealed the briefest twitch, and it satisfied me deeply, like scratching an itch in my lungs. It never took very much. Twenty-year-olds are still children.

I continued my rant. "I can spot a complacent intellect as quickly as I can determine a weak argument—by the end of the first sentence. So make your intentions clear. Life is too short, and this tuition too expensive, to waste anyone's time."

Taylor was still too prideful then to start writing, but she did pick up her pen. Everyone stared, rapt, including me. What other way can I say this? The picking up of her pen stirred me.

Taylor, with her long, swept bangs and hair cut short at the back, her rainbow earring and oversized boy's jeans, didn't continue to challenge me. In fact, she worked so hard that I would read her papers and feel on the brink of orgasm. The thesis was well thought through; the arguments, though sometimes faulty, were cited with precision and taken as far as they could go. To read her essays was to have someone kneeling before me, undoing my zipper.

Then came the paper on the photographer Catherine Opie and I couldn't take it anymore. I had to email her.

Taylor,

Your paper "Queer Eye of Opie" is an above satisfactory achievement. We'll discuss more in conference, but I wanted to commend you on taking such an overused topic and turning it into something much deeper. There may be a possibility of publishing this. Let's talk.

—Professor M

The idea of publishing her paper came out in a flurry of passion, and even though it felt good to type it, afterwards I felt a kind of remorse. In the time it took me to stand, assemble my papers, and get my bag, my inbox chimed. Her response was there, like she had been expecting my email with her reply already written, waiting in her Drafts. I pictured her sitting at the computer, ready to send it, finger poised on the mouse, and I started to sweat. I read it, smiling like a goofball.

Dear Prof M, (Prof! So sweet I could hardly stand it.)

I am literally sitting here giddy. I'm looking forward to our conference. I just read Van der Meer's "Tribades on Trial" for Professor Leon's history of sexuality class, and I found our discussion of it pretty boring and am hoping I could start a discourse with you. Let me know if you need it. I can attach it as a pdf.

T.

Here was the moment when I was guilty, the moment when I knew what I was doing. When I knew that my response would make her shift and buckle over her hand.

43

Taylor,

No need to send. I think I have the text on my shelf.

—Professor M

—

That night, when Julia and I had sex, I tried not to think about this exchange, but I felt cold and disconnected, so finally, I pictured the T. at the end of her email, her offer to attach the article as a pdf. I came loudly, holding Julia's head in my hands as I pictured the textbook, edited by John C. Fout, glowing on my shelf, like it had always been waiting for Taylor.

"You're something else tonight," Julia said.

Her hand was inside of me, well past the knuckles, and I twitched, I buckled, like Taylor did over my email. I suppose I could have told Julia then, because then she would have known that what I was doing with Taylor was helping both of us.

—

We sat across from each other awkwardly. She looked at all of the items on my desk: the books I was reading or blurbing, the tchotchkes that Julia had given me, a picture of the two of us on a hike somewhere. I was sweaty and tanned in that photo, wearing a tank top. Julia's long curly hair was pulled over one shoulder. She was the only person in the world who could go on a ten-mile hike and look refreshed, like she'd just showered. Taylor's eyes settled on this photo. I used my finger to direct the angle of the picture a little more towards me.

"I appreciated getting to review that text again. It had been a few years," I offered.

She nodded. She twisted something in her fingers, but it wasn't a tissue. It was brown, soft. A piece of yarn? My phone rang. I bowed my head to her and leaned over to answer it. Taylor stood to leave, but I held my hand up to her. She stayed completely still in the position I had frozen her in. I couldn't look at that, so I swivelled away.

"Hello?" I said. Taylor was still bent. I covered the mouthpiece. "It's my partner, please relax. No, I'm here. I'm with a student in conference." I listened to Julia. Taylor began to play with her earring. "Strawberries sound good. If there isn't enough arugula in the garden let me know."

I worried that I would have to say "I love you," but I didn't. We hung up without a goodbye, like business partners.

"Sorry about that," I said to Taylor. The brown thing was displayed on her knee. She smiled.

"Sounds like a nice dinner."

"It's our anniversary."

"Oh," she said, sitting up a little more. "Congratulations."

"What are your thoughts on this essay?" I asked.

She held up the brown thing. "I have a little gift for you," she said. "I noticed how your pens are always all over the place in your bag, so I knitted you this thing. So you know where your pens are."

It was unevenly knitted, but I could see now how it would work. It had a little flap, secured by a button.

"That is so clever," I said. I reached for it and she hesitated before giving it to me. I could feel the tug of her end from my end. The yarn was so soft. I undid the button and put three pens inside.

I held it up to her, like *ta-dah!* And she giggled, probably like she had as a baby. I kept the gift on my desk, underneath my fingers.

"You know the part," she said, "where the villagers are watching the two women have sex through the hole in the attic wall, apparently for hours, and one woman just can't take it anymore and says, 'Haven't you had enough fouling around?' or something?"

"What are you talking about?" I asked.

"In the article. I just found that so striking, and I keep thinking about it. We didn't even touch on that in class, aside from the fact that it was bizarre. There's something about voyeurism, the eye, that I find really haunting." She looked at me for courage to go on, and I leaned forward in my chair, which I never do.

She leaned forward a little, too. "I kind of just want to write a paper on the fact that there is documentation that the villagers watched for four hours. And if that woman hadn't called out, maybe everyone would have kept watching. And there's all these views of queer sex being ugly, but that document proves that, even then, it was—is—quite the opposite." She ran her hand through her hair, and I saw that her cheeks were flushed.

"Quite the opposite." I repeated, knowing it was the wrong thing to do. I glanced at the clock and stood. She jumped to her feet.

"Write it. I'll work on it with you. You can do this for your final paper."

"Really? I know you don't like people to change their topics so late in the semester."

"Don't remind me of that." I grabbed the knitted thing and dropped it in my bag.

She stood still for a moment, and I paused and looked at her, my bag over my shoulder. Her face had a slight chubbiness to it—that puppy softness of youth—and I could see it all over her body. I imagined how it would start to redistribute, or disappear forever, over the next three years. I didn't move to hold her, I didn't quite feel compelled to, but I was curious about the availability of her spirit. If I held her in that office, would I feel it on the sides of her thighs, around her ribs? What is it like for someone with a spirit so available to hold someone like me? Am I a heavy, cold thing? Boris at least appeared to love me. The longing in Taylor's eyes was so present. I looked away.

"I have a bus to catch," I said.

I opened the door. I'd never seen anyone move so slowly.

—

I arrived home with my arms full of groceries. I felt lavish after my meeting with Taylor—or maybe guilty—so I bought cheeses and chocolate. I bought a smoked trout spread to have alongside our salads. Boris and Julia greeted me at the door. Boris whimpered, her back claws clattering as she jumped into the air. Midway, she remembered not to put her paws on me and tilted back down to the floor. The house was warm and sunny, fabric and leather strips strewn over the furniture, the sewing machine out on the coffee table.

"I'm sorry about the mess," Julia said. She fixed the bobby pin that kept back the wily piece of hair she was always tugging at, then took the bundle of groceries from my arms. I followed her into the kitchen.

"I decided to start a new shoulder bag for you. You've officially been carrying that one for seven years, and I'm much better than I was then. Look."

47

I followed her to the counter, where the bag rested. She was using the leather we'd bought from a lesbian couple on our block who sold skins.

"See that?" she pointed to a small pocket in the lining of the bag. "That's for your pens. After I gave you the old bag, I was mortified because you'd come to class and I would watch you go searching for pens. They were all loose, and I just couldn't believe I hadn't considered that. I thought, *My God, I'll never be a theorist—I don't need to see everything and how it works so clearly. Let me just be surprised.*" She wrapped her arms around me and kissed me deeply. I tasted onions. I ran my fingers through her hair and brought my lips to her ear.

"I thought you dropped out because of all the Foucault." I felt a ripple through her body.

"Foucault," I said again.

"Stop it." She pinched my side.

The table by the back window was set formally. She opened the wine and I realized I had seen her open probably hundreds of bottles of wine, and every time, I still stared in awe at her hands, the way the fingers made every action seem like a rare skill. This was the kind of thing I had tried not to notice when she was a student, but no matter how hard I tried, I could still see her hands moving, with that pen, moving.

"Foucault was part of it, but it was also just too painful to see you use that bag while you still felt so unattainable. That seems so long ago. I don't think I've felt that kind of awe about you for years. It's nice how things shift."

I put Boris's front paws up on the chair and rubbed down the sides of her body. I stared at the blood spots on her eye and kissed the top of her snout.

"We're coming up on seven years for Boris, too," I said.

"I think that's when I knew we were really together," she said. "That I wasn't just this kid you passed notes with through campus mail. It blew my mind—I was living with you and we had a dog."

I took a sliver of trout and let Boris lick it off my finger.

—

I brought the knitted case back to school and left it in my desk. I did not take it with me to class. Taylor noticed my new bag, saw the pocket where my pens were kept. I didn't make eye contact with her until I was settled. She did not send me an annotated bibliography or consult me about her project again. In fact, on the last day of the term, she didn't hand anything in. She was the first to leave class, and I felt a flash of anger as she walked out the door. *Nothing happened between us!* I wanted to shout at her. The only thing I almost said out loud then—as I felt my head rush with rage—was *Act like an adult.*

I was fuming when I got back to my office. I tossed the final papers on my desk and paced. What made her think that just because I was going to help her with a paper, because I appreciated her work, I would give up my life for her? How dare she be so petty as to not hand in that paper?

I found myself at the computer. My fingers flew on the keys and I couldn't stop. *How dare you?* I wrote. *To act slighted when nothing happened. To think that anything would happen.* I typed and typed. I noticed a red squiggly line underneath one of the words, and then a green squiggly line under a sentence fragment, but I just kept going. I clicked save and then sped out of my office to get home in time to take Julia out to dinner.

49

Later that evening, I stripped down to a T-shirt and sat with a beer to read through the email, only there was nothing in my Drafts folder.

The beer swam thinly in my belly. I opened my Sent folder and there it was, delivered that afternoon when I thought I'd saved it. No subject, no salutation, no closing. The email was enraged and unhinged. I glanced at the first few lines and wanted to disintegrate.

"M," Julia called. "I'm on the phone with Max. Do we have plans Saturday?"

I couldn't answer. What was Saturday? How could I fix this?

I went back to my inbox and there in bold was Taylor's name. The damn RE:. My cursor hovered over it. I wanted a meteor to land right then, right over Silicon Valley, or wherever it was that the internet lived, and shut it down, make it gone for good.

"M?" Julia called again.

I couldn't wait for the meteor to fall. I double-clicked.

> At first I was going to write that I was sorry because no one had ever sent me an email so mean. I think you should know that it hurt my feelings so much that it made me cry. I've been feeling confused about what it means to be a theorist. It seems like a theorist's brain, after reading so much but not actually DOING anything, would just self-destruct one day, which maybe is what yours just did?
>
> I was going to apologize, but now I'm not going to. What you said to me was inappropriate and should be reported because you did lead me on. No one else got comments on their papers the way that I did. No one else got an uninvited

email from you. I know how to read this and you're just as bad as those fiction authors you talked about who claim they are not accountable for what their work does because they are just making art, when the fact is that you were fulfilling the role of seducer and I was fulfilling the role of seduced.

Maybe I'm not a theorist after all. I'm too used to feeling things.

I'm not going to tell anyone about this email, but I do want you to give me an Incomplete and sign me into an independent study with Professor Leon. He and I both think we could count it for the credits your class would have filled.

If you didn't want the pen holder, you should have said it wasn't your style and no thank you.

Taylor Fisher

"Is this a joke?" Julia was standing behind me, her cellphone clutched to the base of her throat.

"A misunderstanding," I said.

I shouldn't have been so cavalier in that moment with her, but since I hadn't heard her come up behind me, I figured she'd only had enough time to infer that a student was upset about a grade or a deadline, the way students often are.

I stood up slowly and looked at her. She hung up the phone. Her fists were clenched. Is it fair to say that in seven years I had never seen Julia's fists clench? And that fact struck me as odd, even as her hands struck me as beautiful. She pushed a fist into my chest. Lightly. I could tell she wanted to push harder.

51

"She gave you a pen holder?"

"I never used it. This isn't like it was with us."

She wasn't breathing and her eyes looked angry. I didn't know that her eyes could look that way, and I wanted them to look at me softly, but I knew, staring into them, that I would never feel that from her again. That was the first thing that made me cry.

"I used your bag when you gave it to me back then. I didn't use her case. I only wrote to her once about a paper. She acted like something more had happened and her entitlement made me mad."

I couldn't stop weeping—a hysterical cry, terrible whinnying sounds on my inhale. Julia was calm. Then I saw her breath heave in, and that made me feel better, but she returned to her stony self.

"Back then, I knew you had a reputation, but I thought I was the only one—"

"You were. You are. I promise."

"How many students?"

"None. This isn't even a thing that happened."

"It was such a risk to be with you," she said. She rubbed at her eye, and I moved to hold her, but she put her hand up, the way I'd done when I asked Taylor to wait for me to finish my phone call. I would have stayed frozen like that forever if it would have made a difference.

"Write her an apology, and then please go, please leave. I don't think I can be in the house with you right now."

—

Every time I came back to the house to get more things, I hoped Julia would change her mind, but each time she seemed more withdrawn, as if she had never seen anything worth anything in me. She called me a sex addict, said she'd read about it for a few hours on the internet and thought I should get help.

"It's your relationship with power," she said.

There was one box of books left and this time we arranged it so she wouldn't be home. When I turned the key, which I was instructed to leave on the kitchen table, I heard Boris whimpering, her claws on the door. I let her put her paws on me, knelt down, and hugged her. I moved her front legs over my shoulders. I felt a swell of affection for Julia. This was not something that she had to do.

My box was by the door, with a note on top of it. At what point would her handwriting no longer be the most intimate, most familiar thing to me?

Take Boris for this month. We'll figure out next month.

—J

Next to the box were Boris's belongings: her bowl, her leash, her bed. I jumped up with the most joy I'd felt in years. Boris spun around in circles, her nails clicking like fireworks.

In the car, we settled in next to each other. Boris rested her head on my lap. I don't know if either of us could feel my spirit—I'm not certain theorists have one—but I felt soft and available. I felt free, knowing that, in the end, Julia and I, at least in this one thing, acted in opposition to how we were set up to act. This is a theorist's happy ending.

the boy on the periphery of the world

I'm totally one of those boys who snaps pictures of himself with his boyfriend's dog as if he were my dog, even though the chances of that ever being true are slim, since Brian won't move in with me. Brian has a boxer named Geraldine, and sometimes when Brian's in class I like to take her for a walk. People say things like "What a sweet girl" or "Your dog is awesome," and I always feel so proud. Sometimes, I'll show off by giving Geraldine commands.

"Wait," I'll say at street corners. She waits and I can tell that, inside, she is just raring to go, but I'll hold off a little longer, her body almost trembling with desire, until I say, "Okay!" And she just goes, and I'll glance at the approving nod of another nearby pedestrian. On these walks, people look at me and think, *There's a typical blond Carolina boy with a well-trained dog.* Maybe they think, *He has a girlfriend and he's thinking of proposing.*

I've already proposed to Brian. He said no.

I thought that was the end of our relationship, and I knelt on the floor of his dorm room and cried. I had just moved into the apartments off-campus the night before and I was already struck by our life differences. The dorm's smell and unyielding faux-wood furniture depressed me. *We are in different life stages*, I thought to myself. But then Brian mussed my hair and knelt down beside me.

"James, I just don't want to get married now. Let's wait until after next summer. We'll live together. See how things go."

In many ways this was a relief. It occurred to me afterwards that I would have felt embarrassed to tell my family, because they wouldn't exactly be excited. Even if they acted excited, there would be part of them that was disappointed. They would think, *This is for real*. It's like all these years I've had my family at a curb, and I've been saying, *Wait, wait, wait*, and they would finally realize that I'm not going to say, *Okay*.

It's been two summers since I proposed to Brian and we aren't living together. Last semester, he decided to get a place of his own, and he brought Geraldine with him.

"My uncle tells me that we have our whole lives to live together," he said. "And that we should enjoy some time living on our own." I watched him scratch up and down the sides of Geraldine's greasy neck. "This summer, for sure," he said.

—

I walk Geraldine back to my apartment, where Brian is supposed to meet me. We're going to a benefit with his uncle, who is also gay. He lives in New York and gives money to a Southern AIDS alliance, and he bought us all tickets. He told us this was a nice chance to get to meet a lot of old queens. When Brian mentioned that I hadn't met any old queens before, his uncle couldn't believe it. I feel totally disconnected from the older generation and, honestly, a little afraid of them.

My uncle died when I was seven and he already seemed so old, though I don't think he'd even turned thirty. When my mom and I visited him in the hospital—which turned out to be the last time I saw him alive—there were clusters of men standing inside his room and milling around outside. There was a kind of damp sound to their voices. It wasn't exactly like they had been crying but like they were soggy. If you left the cushions on the chairs outside and then it rained—these men seemed like those cushions. I remember thinking their skin seemed sort of spongy. It wasn't because they were sick, though very possibly some of them were. My uncle's skin was jaundiced and dry. I imagined squeezing the arms of one of the men over my uncle, wringing out whatever moisture was there and giving it to him. I thought saving him and ending my mother's pain might be as simple as that.

We walked into the room and a few of the men kept talking, except for one heavy, moustached, non-damp–looking guy. My mom held on to my hand tightly as she kissed this man, who had a smile that made me feel really warm and safe. He extended his hand to me, and when I shook it, I felt her hold me tighter. Maybe she already knew then. Maybe she was afraid that if she let me go, I'd float away with the other men as they tided out of the room.

"Luke," he said to me, and then pointed to someone who I understand now was probably his lover: "Aaron."

Luke had a hoop earring like my uncle did. A golden cross dangled from my uncle's, and one time I made the mistake of

57

trying to pull it out of his ear. Uncle Jim screamed and threw me down. I don't think I hurt him that badly, but there might have been a drop of blood. He called for my mom and started to cry. My mom told him not to worry, that there was no way anything could have happened, but I could tell by the rough way she washed my hands that she felt otherwise.

"Uncle Jim doesn't feel well sometimes, so you shouldn't pull on his earring," she explained.

Afterwards, my hands were raw, and my mom, rather than using lotion because all she had was her pretty-smelling stuff, coated them in Vaseline. I doubt she thought that she was preparing me to fist the world. When she wasn't looking, I wiped the gook off on the side of the couch.

Luke saw me staring at his earring and winked. "Your uncle gave it to me today. Told me I had to start trusting in the Lord," he said, gently flicking the cross with his nail.

I looked over at the hospital bed, and Uncle Jim, blind at this point, faced blankly in my direction. His ear was empty.

"I can't touch the earring," I said.

My mom shook my arm and looked like she wanted me to disappear. Or she wanted to disappear. I'm not sure. Luke looked like the kind of person who was always forgiving someone. It was like he'd spent his whole life doing this, as an obligation.

"Young men have to listen to their mamas," he said, and then walked over to my uncle and kissed his temple, the skin as thin as paper. He and Aaron left us alone.

I didn't want to stay long. Maybe it was because I knew my uncle was dying and the room had that strange rotting smell. Maybe it was because I knew my father didn't want us to come and my grandmother had made a point of not going. What I feel now, and was maybe a part of what I felt then, is that I hated

58

keeping those men—his real family—out of the room, away from my uncle.

So maybe I lied. I had met old queens before. They just weren't old when I met them.

—

Inside my apartment, I pull on a pair of Brian's basketball shorts and Geraldine and I get on the bed to begin our photo shoot: moody looks directly into the camera, despondent looks out to the edges of the frame. There is a lovely one of us gazing into each other's eyes, and a candid shot of her resting her head on my chest. I post them all online and text the last one to Brian. A few moments later, my phone buzzes.

Put clothes on. We're coming over.

I'm dressed, I type back. *My suit coat's off.*

I jump up and wash under my armpits, under my balls, and my ass. I splash cold water on my face. By the time I hear footsteps on the stairs outside I am lacing my shoes. Brian knocks first before using the key.

I kiss him on the cheek. His bald, shiny uncle steps in like he has been to my apartment dozens of times. Even though he's totally in his fifties, he looks tightly put together. I notice that the green rim of his eyeglasses matches a strip along the edge of his dress shoes.

"Rick." He shakes my hand slowly as he gazes around the living room. "Well, aren't you two an image of domesticity?"

"I don't live here," Brian says quickly. He pats his leg and Geraldine jumps off the bed and runs to him.

"We're going to move in together next summer, once Brian finishes school," I say.

"Being monogamous so young is like dancing on the periphery of the world, don't you think?"

Neither of us answers.

Rick kneels down to massage Geraldine's neck. She sighs and steps towards him.

"And you, sir," he says, looking up at me. "Congratulations on your graduation. What's next?"

I look down at my outfit and notice a smudged fingerprint on my belt buckle. I'm afraid Rick will think it's Brian's. I rub at it with my jacket.

"Navel-gazing, buckle-shining?" He winks at me, and my face feels hot and swollen. I can't imagine my uncle Jim being this way.

"Summer just started, so I'm going to see how it goes."

Rick is bored by this response. And with that, we decide not to like each other.

"James may have work with a law firm in August, and he might work there for a year. They said they would be interested in putting him through law school if that was the direction he wanted to go," Brian says.

Rick laughs and wipes his shiny head like it is made of money and you can always use more. "If you're going to be a rich one, I suppose he can hang on to you."

—

The drive is embarrassing because Rick insists on sitting in the back seat and I feel like I don't deserve this space in the passenger seat, like I've overridden family. Rick is oblivious, gazing out the window with his sunglasses on. Brian touches my knee. Would I cover his hand with my own if Uncle Jim were in the back seat?

Probably. Brian's hand rests there, without mine, for the whole ride, pulling away instinctively when we reach the valet. I spot the attendant's AIDS ribbon and realize I have forgotten mine.

I pick a ribbon out of the bowl on the valet stand, but Rick plucks it out of my hand and insists on pinning it on me. I've never had another man, aside from Brian, this close to me, this attentive, working his fingers, smoothing the lapel of my jacket.

"So when we leave tonight, we each need to give him a nice tip. Did you bring cash?"

I nod, but Brian says nothing. Rick is still working on me and I'm enjoying looking up at his face, which is actually quite handsome.

"The valet attendants and the servers are all clients of the alliance's centre for the homeless, so it is an unspoken rule that we take care of them tonight."

I try to nod like I know, like this doesn't faze me. I try to picture Uncle Jim as the attendant, and for a second, I see him at his healthiest, saying hello jovially, opening the door with a flourish, bowing, flipping the key in his hand like someone out of an eighties movie. I imagine him taking a Corvette for a joyride with Luke—cigarettes in their mouths, Uncle Jim's hand crawling up Luke's thigh.

Inside, the men wear some of the nicest suits I've ever seen. Aside from the one gay bar in town, I've never been in a room with so many men.

—

When I first met Brian, we were excited to learn we both had gay uncles, who tested positive at the same time, even if their outcomes were different.

61

"Rick was involved in ACT UP. He threw himself on the ground and got arrested and stuff," Brian told me. It was one of our first afternoons together and we lay next to each other in our boxer shorts, Brian's socks still on, the air conditioner humming.

"Maybe our uncles knew each other," he mused, ruffling the hair on my belly.

"I don't know—mine wasn't really out."

"Oh," Brian said. "Sometimes I forget that. It's strange to think about that time 'cause people aren't really dying from it anymore, not like before. You know," he said as he rolled on top of me, "it's amazing that we found each other so early in our lives. We don't have to worry about AIDS or anything, because we'll be together forever. We could even have unprotected sex."

I was still getting used to the feeling of someone else's weight on me, and I had yet to get hard from being scared. He pulled off my boxers, and I placed a leg over his shoulder.

"Probably worth keeping up the practice," I said. "Just, you know, for now."

"Oh, sure," he said. "For now."

—

Uncle Jim was a failure—not a success, like Rick. Standing in this lobby with these men, I feel like a failure, too.

I text my mom: *Uncle Jim's friend Luke. What was his last name?*

I walk over to the bar with Brian and Rick and wait for my phone to buzz. The air conditioning is too high and I'm shivering. The bartender hands me a glass of ice water and it is so cold that holding it hurts my hand.

"Give me a Red Label, neat," Brian says.

I'm surprised and try to catch his eye, but he doesn't look at me. It hadn't occurred to me that I could drink in front of his uncle. I reach into my wallet and put money in the tip jar. I receive a glittery smile from the bartender.

If "people aren't really dying from it anymore," then why are we here? I sip at my water and check my phone while Brian meets Rick's friends. No message yet, just the lock screen photo of me, Brian, and sweet, panting Geraldine on the beach together—Slide to unlock.

I feel Brian's lips at my ear. "He's talking to you." Brian nods to a man about Rick's age with a full head of silver hair. He looks like an executive.

"Sweetie, I was just trying to tell you that you're wearing a beautiful tie."

His finger moves along it nonchalantly, and I feel like the fabric isn't there and it is just his skin on my skin. I can't help but look down at where his finger had been, and the man laughs, grabs Brian's shoulder.

"Oh, he's cute. You locked onto a good one."

At the announcement for us to go to our tables, the phone shakes in my hand: Luke Melville. Sorry, had 2 look it up. Love you, Mom.

I place the awful water on the table and dry my hands on a napkin. "I should have gotten what you got," I whisper to Brian.

"Give me a dollar to tip him and I'll go get you one. I want another one myself."

I hand him the money and realize Rick is watching the whole exchange, leaning back with his hand on his chin and a shitty smile.

"Careful what habits you establish. You're too young for roles yet."

63

I try not to look at him, and run my hands back and forth over my arms, which doesn't create any heat worth talking about.

"It's freezing in here," I say. "I almost feel like I need to step outside to warm up."

"It's always freezing at these events, no matter what time of year. Everyone brings their ghosts with them."

I'm not sure it's possible to understand a word this man says, but I lean in.

"I wonder if you knew my uncle? Jim Fox? He died in eighty-nine."

Rick frowns and shakes his head. He is gazing across the room, looking for someone else to speak to.

"His name sounds familiar, but it might just be a familiar-sounding name."

"What about Luke Melville?"

Now he looks me in the eye. His are a very light blue.

"Of course—we did a lot of organizing together."

"He was my uncle's best friend," I say shyly, uncertain whether I can claim him at all.

"Maybe I remember meeting your uncle—Southern, like Luke but not nearly as charming. First-lovers-cum-best-friends."

A hot water with lemon is placed in front of Rick and I realize I want that much more than a Scotch. He blows on it before taking a sip.

"Luke's still around. He moved out to California. We've lost touch, but I think we're Facebook friends."

He starts scrolling through his phone.

"Here she is. I'll suggest the two of you become friends. Do you have the same last name as your uncle?"

"No—we're related through my mother."

"Well, that's even better. It gives me a reason to send him a message."

I'm tempted to ask what he's writing as his pointer finger moves across the screen, but I resist. That's not what adults do. I can smell Brian's deodorant before he even sits down again. He places the drink in front of me, and it is filled to the top with ice. I thank him, but I don't want to touch it—why can't I get away from this ice? The glass sits there, sweating.

"There's this riddle my uncle told me," I blurt out to the table.

One or two men stop their conversations and look at me, the others keep talking, and the only way I know they are aware I exist is how their eyes dart over at me. I clear my throat.

"I have a riddle," I say, like I'm on the phone with a client who really needs to get the law firm his paperwork, and with that I have the table's attention. Uncle Rick sighs with boredom and I scoot so that I'm angled away from him, even though this means my back is to Brian.

"I don't know if I'm remembering it right. Something like two men each drank a Scotch on the rocks. One was poisoned, the other wasn't. How did he get poisoned?"

"There must be more to the riddle than that," Rick says.

I close my eyes, trying to remember: the rec room on a Sunday, my uncle in front of the TV.

"Well, they were both given the drink at the same time, I think."

"Oh, I know this one," the silver-haired executive says. "They both ordered Scotch on the rocks. One man had to go to a business meeting, so he drank it really fast. The other one died of poisoning because he had nowhere to go, so he savoured his drink over the course of half an hour."

I remember my uncle laughing afterwards—it was "such a puritan riddle," he said. "Protestants always out to scare us for taking pleasure in anything." This idea was more complicated to me than the riddle, which back then made me picture turkeys and weird wide-barrelled guns and men in pilgrim garb drinking Scotch, and the dead one slipping his shoes off under the table as he drinks, and at the thought of those stockinged feet I got this tiny almost-erection, my first. I get it now, the Protestant part, not the erection, here in this cold room.

"It's a real puritan riddle," I say, feeling powerful in their thoughtful silence.

"Oh, I never thought of it that way but absolutely," the executive says, and his eye contact is warm, and I briefly imagine myself in a bathroom stall with him, then out of the stall, in some rest area on I-40 and its 1985—my uncle would have been twenty-two then, like me. The executive has me all the way down his throat, everyone's watching, and there's a thrill—no, it's total joy—I feel in my chest.

"A Catholic riddle," he says, still looking at me.

"Protestant," I say. "Real anti-pleasure."

"Oh, stop it. What do you know about pleasure?" Uncle Rick says.

"The ice!" Brian exclaims.

My whole body twitches at the sound of his voice. I look away from the executive. The bathroom disappears.

"The poison was in the ice. The guy who died let his ice melt."

Someone gives a little golf clap and there's some charmed laughter as Brian coyly lifts a shoulder to his ear.

"Not exactly the most appropriate riddle for tonight. Don't lawyers have a bit more tact? Oh wait," Rick says.

I turn my chair back towards him so fast I almost tip. "Did I, like, do something to you?" I ask. "Because I think I've been nice." And the only thing that keeps me from feeling everyone's discomfort is the relief of giving in to anger.

"Excuse me?" He looks shocked and I know it's bullshit, but I feel myself losing my argument, so I just put my hand around my drink, which has made a wet spot on the table.

"Not the time or place," he says.

Brian's hand squeezes the back of my neck, and I appreciate the attempt, though I don't like how the men at the table are looking at us, like we are a joke. And we are, only having been with each other while, regardless, this ice melts in front of me.

Across from my glass, the executive is still looking at me. He winks, very understated and stylish. Everyone around us communicates in a common language and I don't know the rules. Brian and I fuck, but we aren't gay yet. We tiptoe on the periphery of the world.

The lights dim and men come onstage to give speeches. I hear Brian whisper something to his uncle. I know it's about me, and I don't care to see his uncle's reaction. *First-lovers-cum-best-friends.* Many of the men around us are crying because of what the speaker is saying. This is what it means to be in a room full of ghosts.

My phone buzzes and I check it under the tablecloth, the blue glow radiating out from my lap. I approve Luke Melville's friend request, and there's a message from him: *Your dog is so adorable!*

I reply, *Thanks, but she's not my dog.*

I put my phone away and don't care to see if I've annoyed anyone. I join in on the applause. I sip from my drink.

67

chewbacca and clyde

Meredeth and I never got married. We never even declared that we were monogamous. For all intents and purposes there was nothing that distinguished the first night we got together (feigning obliviousness, drunken on our dorm room floor) from the ten years we spent together. But that didn't make the infidelity hurt any less.

In the beginning we didn't get married because we didn't think about it, it didn't seem to be what queers did, but then when our friends started having commitment ceremonies we thought, *Well, maybe we'll do that next year.* And with every cherries jubilee we made for commitment potluck after commitment potluck, we said, "Us too, next year."

Until we reached eight years, and one night in bed I leaned over and whispered to her, "Let's not bother."

She turned to me with more enthusiasm than she had in quite a while and clutched my hand to her breast.

"Oh, thank God. I don't want to either."

—

Have you ever gotten carried away? Or felt more in touch with yourself than you've felt for a long time, and it's brought on not necessarily by the proximity of another person, or by longing, but by a day of bright, clear sun, or swimming in warm water and feeling the whateverness of your own body?

I found a group on Meetup called Rainbow Rompers who were hosting a queer backpacking trip. I was dangling from the talons of a conversation with my agent earlier that week, who dropped me because my writing was getting "too gay" in a quirky, subversive way, not in a boring, predictable way, not in keeping with my formula.

I'd once been hailed as the Philip Roth of gay and lesbian fiction and my formula was tight. If a gun appeared in the first act, it always went off in the next. A straight character got seduced, a mother came to understand, and a dazzling John Updike finish. Though no one compared me to John Updike, and the only place where I sold anything like Roth, where people bought my books because they felt they should or because I was someone they were supposed to like, was in Seattle and at Bluestockings bookstore in New York. But my agent tells me that neither of those venues are accurate or representative, and that when I talk like this I sound like someone who doesn't quite understand the publishing game trying to critique it anyway.

So Meredeth and I went online. We stared at the photo of the group leader. He exuded a physical masculinity that was much more rugged than my academic sweaters and oversized glasses.

"Yes, do it," Meredeth said, leaning over my shoulder. "I did a similar trip once. This is a beautiful time of year."

She found her old pack in the garage. We checked the tent for holes, the sleeping bag for animal nests.

"You just need some independence," she said.

So I bought a flight to Los Angeles without a companion ticket. I even took a cab to the airport.

—

On the second-to-last day of the trip we hiked fifteen miles, and our bodies were feeling tired and wild and we made it to this lake and it was warm and it didn't look nasty and we stripped off our clothes and jumped in. The sweat had dried to me—my pubic hair was crusty and matted—so it felt amazing to leap around in that water with everyone, and to see all of these variant bodies in all of their different expressions. It didn't feel shocking when we were sunning ourselves on the rocks and two people started hooking up, and then another two. And it didn't feel like the pairing off that happens at spin the bottle parties. This was like rubbing on suntan lotion. This was like we were all included. So when this person pressed his mouth to my thigh, and then to my clit, I just stretched back and felt the rush of how beautiful this all was, how this is what things should be like, all of us here, together, enjoying each other with ease. I felt alive in the same way I had the first time I had sober sex.

"What a goddamn gift," I said out loud, and everyone around me murmured or chuckled.

Guilt didn't set in after I came. Or at the airport. It didn't set in when Meredeth picked me up and I held her close to me in the car. *The world*, I thought, *is so beautiful and capable and full*

71

of illusion. So the first thing I told her about, once I was home, before I even showered, was what had happened on the beach. And still, no guilt, even when she looked at me like I was insane, her delicate mouth gaping open. Though I did stutter when she leaned against the wall for support, I was still talking when she came at me, punched me in the shoulder, and then cried out, "Is this true? You're talking like you're in a fucking cult."

That was when I started to feel whatever stability or bliss I had slip away, just as night terrors do when one wakes suddenly and the conviction that the monster is in the kitchen dissolves. I was left with this fractured certainty. I rubbed my shoulder.

"I didn't think that—"

"Who are you?" she asked.

She fell to the ground and started to sob, and I felt everything I'd ever wanted zip out past me—one, two, three—towards the window, but I couldn't grab any of it because this person I loved was now so far away from me.

"You don't even feel bad!" she cried.

She barely made it to the bathroom, where I held her hair while she vomited and the last of the euphoria, and the last of my safety, escaped out the window.

—

The rules of heterosexuality draped over us like a shroud, and in the dark, everything happened quickly: splitting our bank account, giving notice to our landlord. She changed her relationship status on Facebook to single and we started getting wall posts and phone calls. We were still living in the same house when she unfriended me.

72

"At night, I can't sleep and I obsessively search through your friends to see if any of those people have been added, and I just can't put myself in that position anymore."

"I haven't added any friends. I'm not ready for this to be over," I pleaded.

"I can't believe you're doing this," she said.

"I'm not doing anything. I want to be with you."

I knelt down in front of her and there was this moment when it felt like everything would soften, everything would be okay. She ran her fingers over my head. I always kept the back clipped close to the neck but let the top grow full, and sometimes she would laugh and gel it into Italian gangster hairdos. The first time she did this was for a costume party, and I thought we were going to end up doing something very butch-femme: she Bonnie, me Clyde. Instead, she showed up in a gigantic Chewbacca costume, which took the power away from mine (suddenly, I was just a 1930s-era butch with a gun). I was certain there would never be anyone else for me.

I watched her as she stroked my hair and I saw the Chewbacca within her. I wanted so badly to just be Clyde and Chewbacca, because I knew they would not have this problem. Clyde and Chewbacca, if they were together in this apartment, would have let it all go.

"Let's try something," I said.

"I don't want to try anything."

I grabbed her hand and pulled her towards the bedroom. I was so excited, so desperate. There was no doubt in my mind that this would work.

She snapped her hand away. "I will not have sex with you."

"That's not what I'm trying to do."

73

I pulled out a box of costumes and the Chewbacca one was near the bottom, squished to the side, looking a little bald in places, as if the costume had aged like we had. I unfolded the Clyde outfit, but I couldn't find the gun.

"Here," I said, throwing the costume at her. "Put this on."

"No."

"Please, just do this so that we can at least say we tried."

While she struggled into the Chewbacca suit, I pulled on my pants and snapped the suspenders. I grabbed some pomade out of the bathroom cabinet and came back to the bedroom to do my hair in front of our mirror. I didn't want to leave her alone. Already I could sense her slipping away; her physical body was the only thing that hadn't gone.

"You'll need to zip me," she said, holding a mass of fluff together at the back.

There was something reptilian about the knots in her spine within the folds of all that fur, and I tried not to make it obvious how slowly I was going. I wanted to remember the disappearance of each vertebra.

"It smells in here," she said, her voice amplified by the plastic around the mouth.

"Here, let's stand in front of the mirror."

My hand was sticky with gel and I felt it catch on her paw. She pulled away and adjusted the Chewbacca head, which kept dipping down so that the eye holes fell at her cheeks.

"Here we are," I said.

We stood staring at ourselves.

"You don't look like anything," she said. "You just look like a dyke." She clutched at the back of her costume. "Can you unzip me? I feel like I'm going to pass out."

74   "I want to say something first, while we're like this."

"But I'm seriously going to pass out."

"We didn't have any rules."

"Get me out of this," she said.

"We didn't have any rules," I repeated. "And what would have happened if we did?"

She brought her hands to the mouth to pry the jaws open and the plastic snapped. I quickly reached behind her, but a quarter of the way down, the zipper got caught on the fur.

"Hurry up!" she shouted.

"I'm trying not to rip it."

"Rip it. I'm not going to wear this fucking thing again."

"Yes, you are."

She pushed me away and pulled her arms out of Chewbacca's arms, back into herself, and then in some sort of gymnastic feat, she tore the costume at the zipper enough to get her head out. She looked new and sweaty, and I could tell that she'd been crying, but I didn't think it was over me or our costumes. She shimmied out and kicked the fur in my direction.

"Maybe I would have tried harder to get over it," she said. "But maybe you wouldn't have thought it was okay to fuck around."

"But we still don't have any rules. We don't have to break up. We can get through this, because there's nothing telling us that this has to end us."

"Maybe I just don't want to try," she said. She began to put on her normal clothes. Her flesh disappeared, like a quarter found, then lost again behind an ear. "If you could have just said that you felt bad, or guilty—maybe. But this is just, you know, too little."

I mussed my hair and it stuck straight up. I slid my suspenders down my arms. "If you had been there, you would understand why it didn't feel wrong."

"So I'm not queer enough?" she asked, and I could feel it starting again. We would never stop doing this until one of us was gone.

"I wish we could fix this with a baby or something."

Maybe one day, I could tell the kid about what I had done and show them there is another way to feel about things. And for a second I saw us, with a child that looked like someone else, a photo of a person whose face we'd forgotten. Our arms around each other, and the baby, with little Chewbacca slippers and suspenders, holding a water pistol shaped like a dolphin because we wouldn't want the baby to play with anything that looked like a gun.

the appropriate weight

My daughter fell apart while reading a poem. I sat in the back of the church because I didn't want anyone to see me walk in, but at the moment she began crying I felt the strangeness of it, that if she were a little girl, I would be running to her side and catching her as she left the altar. But there was no way I was going to run up the long aisle now, letting shame trail behind me (which I wore out of habit for those present). This was different from your kids growing up. There are things you lose the right to do when you are no longer the one married to the deceased.

My ex-wife Miriam's current husband replaced my daughter at the pulpit. He was barrel-chested, wore a diamond ring on his pinky that caught the afternoon light and flashed at us like a satellite at night. He looked more con man than journalist. I didn't know that was something my ex-wife would like: Neil

Diamond tapes ringing through his Ford Taurus, gin and tonics and playing cards, and her legs straight up in the air as they fucked. That is one of the rights I've lost—thinking about my ex-wife in that way. We mostly had sex missionary, but then, we were so young. I hadn't had sex with anyone before, and neither had Miriam. No one told us much about what to do, so it felt lucky that we were able to figure it out and have orgasms. She orgasmed throughout our marriage, which, if I could give a eulogy, I would say. But that wouldn't be for her benefit; it would be for mine. When her friends and family see me, they think about a life of not being loved, a life without any passion. They imagine me lying on top of her, my muscles tensed, unable to stay hard. It was never like that, but I realized in a bar bathroom late one night, in the final months of our marriage, that there was an opportunity for a very different kind of passion.

Oh, you're thinking, I *get* it *now*. Like her family members did. My inability to carve a turkey made sense to them, and my irritability with their boring stories, and my nice shoes, and her nice shoes, and our clean house, and our dachshund, Murray, who loved me best, and our one gay child, who I'm not certain thinks of me at all.

Miriam's husband bowed his head, restrained a sob, and though I hoped to leave before he was done speaking, the church was so quiet that even the shifting of seats would be a disturbance. There was no movement, just the sniffs of those around us, which sounded eerily like shutter clicks. Imagine our grief as photo ops. For a brief period, that's what it is, until a few weeks go by and we are still grieving, but there's no place for it anymore. The sob escaped and Miriam was supposed to run up and hold him, but that wasn't going to happen, which sent another sob through him. He stepped away from the podium,

78

looking lost and small, like a child bobbing in the ocean. And though we were all grateful when a young man (maybe his brother or son) stepped forward and caught him in a hug, I knew that he was feeling only weight—too heavy because it wasn't Miriam's weight—and that this man who hugged him was lacking some dip that existed only on her lower back—not the masculine centre of the back—where he would prefer to put his hand. Thus, it was no comfort at all.

I stayed for the recessional. I recognized Miriam's brother as the head pallbearer and saw him look at me, then look away. A few friends acknowledged me grimly. Miriam's husband didn't see me, but my daughter did, and hers was the only face that looked grateful. She might not love me the way Murray does, but she loves me in some deep and tragic way, which doesn't necessarily mean she wants to talk to me.

—

"Sal's a cunt man, and he wants it all over him," Miriam said to me on the phone soon after she started dating the journalist/gangster, while we were finalizing some logistics around the divorce.

I imagined him slick like a seal, their bodies slipping off of each other—joyous in all their fluids—and the bed a mess. I, too, was learning that the best sex was not tidy: the shit and cum and odour were part of what felt so good—to be an animal, to be loved as an animal, to the full extent of your body, thus reaching your soul. The filth meant fucking on an energetic level. It's because Miriam said things like "Sal is a cunt man" that her family thinks I was an icy ruiner. But she hadn't awoken me either.

"I got a question for you, if I may," she said.

I heard her take a long drag from her cigarette while I deliberated. Technically, we weren't supposed to be talking to each other—our lawyers had suggested that all correspondence go through them—but we had been together for nearly thirty years and we couldn't help it, like her fingers sliding to the pack for a cigarette before the current one was finished.

"Are you ... I'm not sure of the term ... Are you the man or the woman?"

I groaned, and she started to laugh.

"Don't be so PC. Do you take it or do you give it?"

I hadn't agreed to be asked the question yet, so I bought time by clearing my throat and taking a long drink of water.

"Don't tell me you're too shy to answer this."

"Don't tell me," I said, "that a few fucks from a meathead made you a bigot."

"Make me less of one," she said. "C'mon, you know I mean well. I don't know the terms."

"The term's 'bottom,'" I said, "but it's not always about penetration."

I wanted to say more about what it meant to be opened like that, the vulnerability and the weight and the pain—at the beginning and sometimes still—and the sheer disbelief that I was a space for claiming and fitting. She would have understood, but I was never that blunt with her. It was always this way—her expressiveness with me, and my restraint. Why change it now?

I will recognize the sound of her inhale from a new cigarette when her spirit hovers over me on the day I die (unless the right of a final visitation has also been stripped from ex-husbands; I'm not certain of the rules).

She laughed and I heard the smoke hiss out of her lungs. "I know what you mean. It's that way with us, too."

—

I waited in my car in front of the restaurant where the backroom was reserved for the reception. It didn't seem right that I should be the first one there, but neither did I want to enter a crowded room. I wanted to hug my daughter, shake hands with a few old friends, and then escape out the back, my mouth tasting of salami and olives. Boredom finally sent me out of my car and into the backroom, where the wait staff were just putting out the first finger foods. They are invisible in much the same way I was invisible in the church. It's the term "wait staff" that does it, kind of like "ex" in my case. They bustled around and pretended not to see me. I hovered behind them and made myself a plate of provolone and salami and artichoke hearts. I placed my little plate on a table when a few people started to filter in, including two old friends, a couple we used to have over for dinner. The husband, who was the Latin teacher at the school where Miriam taught language arts, had aged in the ten years since I'd seen him. His fit body (yes, I noticed back then) had given way to something pouchy and loose. His wife kissed both my cheeks and the husband took both my hands in his.

"We were hoping we'd see you today, but we weren't sure." The sound of his voice was like that inhale of Miriam's cigarette. Standing with these two old friends in this new setting, with these new lives—I wasn't sure what to say.

"Is your friend here?" the wife asked, and her husband gave her a look, which I didn't know how to interpret: *We don't know whether they are still together* or *It's not appropriate for him to bring him?* I had thought the latter and told Dale it would be best if he stayed home.

81

"Dale stayed back in New Hope," I said, feeling like the place where I lived was a cliché of rainbow flags and late-in-life come-outs and bi-curious teenagers—which it was.

His wife gave me a look of pity. "It would have been okay to bring him."

"I didn't think it would be appropriate. Besides, he had to work." The former a truth, the latter a lie.

They nodded and the talk was forced for a time, until either the husband or I said something that made us all laugh and we were great friends, minus one, and in the wrong setting.

Others arrived, including my daughter, who approached the three of us immediately. She looked like her mother had at her father's funeral—her hair thin and pulled back tight, her face pale without makeup. The girls she dated always looked just like her—femme but in a softball-tour-bus kind of way.

Once, while she was in college, not long after she came out, she asked, in the blunt manner of her mother: "Do you identify more with being gay or queer?"

A younger boyfriend had explained his version of the difference to me, after I told him that my attraction had less to do with genitals and more to do with the way I was handled and what he called my expansive desire, and that I listened to *Democracy Now!* So I didn't have to think about my answer to this question for very long.

"Queer," I said.

She rolled her eyes, and I had to prompt her a few times before she'd say anything more.

"I shouldn't get annoyed when you say it. Men can't understand feminist liberation."

I didn't like that she called me a man, but I didn't have the language then and don't quite still.

"So you're a—" and I waved my hand in the air a few times, waiting for the reveal.

"You can't even say it," she said, her voice trembling with hurt. "I'm a lesbian. You can't even say it."

I slipped my arm over her shoulders and she surprised me by wrapping her arms around my waist. I kissed her lesbian head, and my friends excused themselves to the buffet, plentiful now with baked ziti and meatballs.

"Where's Dale?"

"Couldn't make it," I said.

I offered my plate to her, but she shook her head. So I took a bite of cheese and then offered the cheese to her and she took it. I took a bite of artichoke and then offered the artichoke to her and she took it. Certain rules, long established, stay the same. One or two of Miriam's family members came over to say hello, but they didn't ask about Dale. While I made small talk with them, I continued to feed my daughter until all that was left was an olive, which I popped in my mouth because she doesn't like them.

When my daughter stepped away to speak with Sal's daughter —"Closeted," she whispered to me, "I know it"—I was alone in the middle of the room, but I felt like I could pass through the people around me, that I didn't look small and swimmy, as Sal had near the altar. Sal wasn't there yet. I tossed my plate away and decided to make a fairly quiet exit through the back door. I hugged my friends goodbye, the oil from the salami and the olives fresh on all of our lips. I blew a kiss to my daughter.

In the parking lot I noticed the sun, and that my hand made contact with the stair railing but didn't pass through it. Sal was leaning against the back of his SUV. He saw me, and I wasn't certain whether I was supposed to see him, but I walked towards him anyway.

I'd had a fantasy on the drive to the funeral that a moment like this would happen. That we would be alone, and somehow we would end up in his car, which I had imagined was much like the car he leaned on now. Miriam and I had always been about the same size and I was curious to feel my body in that passenger seat, taking up her shape. And then something sexual would happen that neither Sal nor I would claim to understand but that both of us needed, as if we could swim through the fluids of our own bodies towards Miriam.

We shook hands, and I was surprised that my grip was much stronger than his. We each stated the other's name. Murray often needed to be reminded of himself when I came home from work, and the shock of my hand on his ears or head always caused him to pee on the floor, as if through this explosion of fluid he could claim once again that he existed. Sal and I stood silently for a few moments, in our mutual existence.

"I'm sorry for your loss," I said—a line from a script—uncertain what I meant by it, or what it meant, the words sounding like another language in my mouth.

"Thanks," he said.

We stood there like people who have something in common that neither really wants to bring up, until he tried. "My ex-wife is gay, too."

"Okay," I said.

Sal put his hand out again, and I waited until it was fully extended before I reached for it. Just before the building door creaked, I imagined his body, slick like a seal, in a tiny bar's bathroom late at night, and I saw my body, split open and opening more than I could ever imagine, on a ruined bed.

And just before Sal pulled his hand away and trotted over to whoever was coming outside, I heard Miriam inhale, the smoke filling my lungs, and his lungs, and lucky for me, Dale's lungs. He would exhale into my mouth when I came home and offer me the appropriate weight when I collapsed into his arms.

ninety days

"Were you having trouble breathing last night or something?"

It was early. Denise and I were still in bed. I gave a little half shrug that I often thought was adorable, but there was no indication that it was received that way. I tried to stop looking cute and speak in an adult-sounding voice—not the childlike voice I habitually used with Denise.

"Not that I noticed. Why?"

Denise sat up and pulled on a T-shirt. I watched breasts disappear and was disappointed, even though those breasts had become like strangers to me. For the past year, in addition to avoiding pronouns, or using "they" instead of "he" or "she," Denise had asked me to pretend they—the breasts in this case—didn't exist, to not touch them anymore, to not sexualize them, because they were confusing. I obeyed because I loved and respected Denise, and also because it felt sexy to have something that I couldn't do. But by putting that shirt on, Denise had shut the door to sex.

"You were doing that thing where you kind of chortle and breathe through your mouth again. It sounds like you're choking."

They slammed the covers to the side and roughly got out of bed, and in the process their fist sort of hit my hip bone. It hurt a little, but I decided not to feel it since Denise hadn't noticed they'd done anything.

"Sorry about that," I said. I put on a T-shirt and covered my own breasts, aware that no one was sad to see them go.

At the end of the bed, Denise stopped moving abruptly. "I can't imagine living with that sound for the rest of my life."

There was no sense of remorse in that face, probably because it was so full of truth. I do make a weird sound at night, and what I wasn't brave enough to ask Denise was: *Isn't it worse during the day when my nose makes a fairly regular whistle on my exhale?* When I came out at twenty-one, my mom—overcome by shock or rage or what she thought she was supposed to do—popped me quickly in the nose. A snap of the wrist. And I remember that as I covered my face, her hands went to her mouth. She let out one sob, then said, "I don't know why I did that. I'm totally fine with this."

"Do you want to help pay for a surgery to fix it?" I asked.

"I got my own body to worry about," Denise said sharply, and it was so early in the morning, it sounded like a shout.

I slipped out of bed and stood on my tiptoes. I was expecting a long fight, and I wanted us to be on equal footing. I wanted Denise to look into my eyes, which didn't happen.

In an instant, Denise broke up with me.

"I've been thinking about this for a while," they said.

"But I haven't."

We let that statement in its powerlessness hang in the air before it dissolved under the high-pitched hiss that escaped my nose, which I wished I could tear off and throw at Denise, who wouldn't even talk to me. They said I was being petty—wanting closure, wanting an explanation. It was capitalist, they said, of me to want a reason. Denise had this ability to be so stoic no matter how upset I got.

I screamed, "What do I need to do to get you to respond to me? Do I need to, like, shit right here in front of you? Right on the rug? Like an animal?"

I moved like I was going to pull my pants down, and even though Denise was looking at me, it wasn't like they were seeing me.

Obviously, I didn't do it.

Denise's best friend, Del, came by with a truck and by the evening had carted them and all their things away.

The last bit of communication I received was a postcard (a picture of our town's waterfront) asking me not to reach out. Denise said we needed to take ninety days of no contact. The only soft thing written on this card was that they thought the ninety days would help me let go and heal.

The pronoun thing wasn't that hard for me. But what's hard about telling this story, with using "they" right now, is that it puts Denise even further away from me. That sense of plurality, that singular they, asserts that Denise doesn't belong to me anymore and never did. This is capitalist. I know this.

—

I'm sensitive about being recognized as queer or radical. As someone assigned female at birth who presents as femme I have to make a series of conscious decisions to be visible as queer, and I still have to come out, multiple times a day. So I don't just wear the barrette, I attach the turquoise giraffe-shaped fascinator and smudge my mascara. Once, just to go to the coffee shop, I spent hours working my hair into a beehive. I wrap fur around my shoulders in the grocery store. I flirt with all the butches and the studs and the ones who prefer to be called masculine-of-centre, even when I don't really want them, because there is little that is more satisfying than watching another queer's shoulders soften as they smile at me excitedly in that open-mouthed way once they know.

I've always dressed this way, though, even before realizing I was queer. It wasn't until I came out that I denied myself in any way. I tried to look moody, morose, and wore little-boy clothes to parties where I scowled and tried not to say much unless it was to concur with some judgment of a person under the guise of condemning a system. No to marriage, yes to labour rights, no to makeup, yes to thrift stores. Yes to smelling a little dusty. Yes to looking mostly male.

The party where I met Denise was where all my stoic butch stuff began to fall apart. I don't even remember what Denise said—and it's possible that I was so starved for my own person-ality and so desperate to express something that it was really only mildly funny—but I let out a squeal after the joke, and everyone looked at me.

"Oh Lord," I said, folding over to prevent all of me from spill-ing out. My voice was loud; my nose whistled.

No one else was laughing—most were eyeing me suspiciously —but I remember Denise smiled. It was playful, exposing, and extended out into the room like an offering of friendship, which I snatched before they could decide otherwise.

Our relationship began subtly. We planned to ride bikes together to the next party and Denise showed up with two masquerade masks, both hot pink with a wild display of feathers. But one mask was also covered with sequins, and this was the one that Denise thought I should wear. I remembered a pair of hot-pink tights I'd abandoned that my mom bought me for a Halloween costume and pulled them on under a pair of torn-up jeans. At some point over the course of the night, I removed the jeans and wore the tights as pants, and though many of the faces at the party remained stoic, quite a few turned to grins.

Then, on a trip to the thrift bins, I found a leopard-print bustier, the wiring a bit warped but otherwise in good condition.

"Look at this," I said to Denise. "It's disgusting what women have trapped themselves with."

I held it up with a finger and felt proud that I had come up with something to say that had a clear critique, and that I thought I kind of agreed with. Denise looked at the bustier, then at me, and just like that first revealing smile, their eyes now also showed what they imagined. And it was me. I knew it was me.

"Yeah, but I think it's kind of sexy."

I added it to my bag, and that night, I biked to Denise's house. By the time the door opened, I'd pulled off my jeans and was standing there in the bustier, the pink tights, and the mask. My hair was teased like eighties metal. Denise didn't smile, but those eyes were the same as they had been that afternoon. From that night on, I externalized desire for Denise. But if they didn't want it anymore, what was I doing?

—

It's hard enough to do ninety days of no contact in a big city—I'd read novels set in New York where lovelorn characters split up Manhattan—but how do you split up a small town? I didn't understand what belonged to either of us here. There was a downtown strip with bars for hunters, and some gems in the strip malls—the Asian grocery, a pet shop window with puppies in it, an antique shop with quirky records—but not enough to divide and claim.

I'm either a little bit psychic or ruled by fear, and it was difficult to determine which was speaking the first morning I felt emotionally capable of getting out of bed and going to the grocery. But I couldn't get the car to head in that direction. It was almost as if I could feel this presence that was Denise—the force halted my car, and even though I pressed my foot on the gas, I couldn't really move. I performed actions I'd learned from other white queers who had appropriated them from cultures they knew no one in: burned herbs around myself and my car, made a little altar with bird bones and feathers on the dash. But maybe that's when fear stepped in, because even as I was waving that bundle of sage in front of me, it didn't clear a thing.

I wasn't certain which friends were still mine during that time, but I tried calling different people to test it out, mostly out of desperation that I not starve to death. I'd try, "Hey, would you mind picking me up milk and a bag of rice?"

"No problem. Do you need anything else?"

"Well," I'd say, glancing into my refrigerator, "since you asked."

This was how I wanted the interaction to go, but typically no one answered, or if they did, I got off the phone angry, wondering why, for instance, Jasper answered just to say nothing, which drove me to ask in a kind of panicked way, "Could you pick something up from the grocery for me?"

"I can't," Jasper said, voice husky, pretending not to be awake yet. "I have band practice."

"Maybe you could take me after band practice?"

"Meeting with that prison reform group."

"What about after that?"

"I don't know when after will be."

What was the point of being in community if you could be so easily thrust from it?

I didn't want to mention any of this to my mom, so for a month I ate what was left in the apartment—lentils, chickpeas, oats, and dry cereal—and in the garden, Denise's garden. I'd watched from the kitchen as Denise lifted each plant out of the earth like nothing had kept them rooted there, as if they had just chosen to be there and now chose otherwise. All that was left were salad greens—probably because they were too difficult for Denise to take with them—and a few varieties of edible flower: borage, violets, and bitter calendula.

I ate these things and looked at myself in the mirror, in sweats, my hair loose. I didn't feel like a femme, or a she, or a he, or a they—I was no gender. I put my hand on my jaw while I chewed and felt it rise and fall as I watched the reflection opposite.

"Can I exist if I'm only in relation to myself?" I asked out loud. My voice sounded hollow and I didn't have an answer.

—

At around thirty-five days I felt something clear. It was like what I knew of Denise had disappeared—picture a body, like in a cartoon, giving a slight pop as it evaporates in a puff of smoke. I was so overwhelmed by grief that I went out to the garden and pushed my hands in the dirt, just to feel something give and

93

yield. It wasn't that the ache I felt for Denise was gone but as though my experience of them was totally gone from the world, or cut off from me.

I got in my car and there was no force or presence. Nothing kept me from anything and I walked right into the grocery store, a bit stunned, and purchased chocolate milk. I felt a kind of empty power course through me as I sipped it, staring at the slow-moving puppies in the pet store window. The Asian grocery had closed since Denise left and a hipster record shop had replaced it. I felt complicit in gentrification as I walked in, but that didn't stop me from listening on headphones to Del's new album and using the reflective back of the CD case to apply more eyeliner. I strolled into the coffee shop, a space I thought I wouldn't walk into again, and familiar faces looked at me and sort of saluted. I felt a surge in my existence. In that moment, my hand shaking as I paid for my coffee, I couldn't even remember the name of the person I mourned. I shook my head, and the barista, whom I knew peripherally, looked startled and maybe a little afraid, so I smiled and turned away. And I would have left if a group of folks I knew hadn't waved me over.

"How are you?" one asked.

I bit the lip of the coffee cup, then looked at the imprint my lipstick left. I wasn't sure if I could say anything without sobbing. I felt so strange.

"How's Denise?" another one asked, and I swear, for a very brief moment, I paused at the name. Someone elbowed that person, who kind of snickered.

"I don't know," I said. "We're not talking."

Someone snorted and they all returned to their original conversation, so I left without saying goodbye. This was how the town had been divided. There had been nothing keeping me from the grocery store—which I nearly developed scurvy from lack of visiting. I could move anywhere I wished, but the friends wouldn't be mine for a while.

When the ninety days were over, I tried calling Denise once. The voice mail greeting had changed—there'd always been sort of a cute and fun recording: "Tell me what it means to be Denise." I loved that recording and always took advantage of it to say it meant being sexy and strong and kind, it meant having great thighs and an incredible tongue. Now there was just an automated voice stating the phone number. I felt panic rise—I didn't know if I should leave a message and thought maybe the sound of my voice would be too upsetting, so I spoke in what I considered to be a British accent.

"G'day! This is your old friend Ana. Been a bloody long time. Miss talking to you, chum."

Then I paused because I wanted to say "I love you" in a normal voice and still didn't know how to say goodbye without it. So I just hung up.

I didn't hear back and I didn't call again.

—

I think the ninety days thing is mostly so the community can reset itself and get used to having two once-partnered people re-enter the group with a somewhat clean slate. It's kind of like using an outdated web browser on an old, slow computer that you don't have the money to upgrade, but the page always refreshes, eventually, and maybe the relief in the end outweighs the frustration.

So the web browser refreshed and Jasper invited me to the prison reform group, and afterwards we made out in the parking lot. Then the barista asked me on a date, and the owner of the record store, and the teenage boy who bagged my groceries. I was asked on so many dates, and sometimes I would even be on a date and get asked on another one. At some point, they always asked me how Denise was, if I'd heard from Denise. When I said no, they would smile, and maybe try to see how many fingers they could put in my mouth.

When I was twelve, my Italian grandpa took me to his Knights of Columbus Hall—they were offering ballroom dance lessons for grandchildren of members. I was the first grandchild to arrive, and I remember the way the other grandfathers smiled when they looked at me; at the time, I didn't interpret it as pervy. The room was warm and blue with cigar smoke. My grandpa lit a cigarette as he set the needle on the record player, while the other men spread into a circle. I danced with one man in the centre, and I felt like I was coasting on ice, my feet barely touching the floor. And then I was passed to another man, and then another, spinning and spinning, until I'd danced with everyone in the room.

A little over a year after the breakup, I ran into Del at the grocery. He seemed to be deciding between oranges based on their heft, one in each hand, and greeted me warmly. I responded in kind and was so amazed that I didn't feel a twinge of fear, and that Del didn't seem to either.

Del's band had been on tour for a while, and now they were finally settled back in town. They'd actually made some money, so he was able to take time off for things like determining an orange's merit by its weight.

"I wish this were how it could always be," Del said, tossing an orange into his cart. "I feel like the person I'm supposed to be." He gave me a very dignified and respectful glance up and then down. "You're looking like a fox."

Del meant literally. I had just died my hair carrot red with some brown stripes along the sides, and I had styled it in a mix of spiky and long. In addition to my fur shrug, I was wearing black pleather leggings and boots that I'd painted to look like back paws. I looked down and adjusted my fur.

"I haven't talked to Denise for a while."

Del didn't say anything. He picked up a mango and sniffed it.

"I was wondering if they moved out of town or something."

"Look, he's probably going to be pissed at me, but go ahead and tell him that I did this."

The pronoun shift would have usually been a familiar indication of what was going on—I heard this all the time in community—but in the moment, I'd forgotten all my politics, was completely daft. Del reached into his pocket, took out an old receipt, and wrote down an address.

"He's been trying to be private about things. He goes by Dane now."

I looked at the address. Dane was living in the country, at the edge of town, which seemed unsafe to me.

"He wanted to tell you, but he wasn't ready yet."

"Does anyone else know?" I asked.

Del pressed his lips together. I thought of my grandpa's lips on his cigarette as he moved the record player's arm.

"Yeah." He lowered his head briefly, and then reversed that movement and lengthened his spine to his full height. I've come to recognize this as the action a progressive person makes before trying to reason with you.

"To his credit, he really got mad at folks when he found out they were asking you where he was, which was partly why he moved to the country. His thinking was if this community was just gonna act like any small town, he didn't want to be part of it."

"They were making fun of me?"

"They were being assholes."

I pictured the men spinning me in the meeting hall but replaced them with the faces of my genderqueer dates, laughing at me, gnawing on this secret while they slid a hand up my thigh.

"He has a new number, too. Let me text it to you."

I watched Del's fingers slide across the screen of his phone like they were moving through heavy cream. I squeezed a mango so hard I put my thumb in it. I buried it beneath the others.

I went outside to a pay phone and dialled the number, knowing he wouldn't pick up the unknown number. The voice mail clicked on, and even though his voice had a deeper drill-whine to it, I could still make out the familiar, tender cadence.

"Dane's not here, but Dane wants to know what's up. Dane wants to take care of your needs."

I hung up. The last part of the message made me think of him dating other people and it was like no time had passed and I hadn't fucked everyone. I felt sick. How to explain the thought of someone not wanting you anymore? How to describe someone erasing you with the same pencil that drew you, leaving only your paws?

—

The house looked nicer than I expected. There was a vegetable garden out front growing our tomato plants and a row of collard greens. A swing hung on the porch, and there was a tool shed at the side of the house where a wheelbarrow rested against the frame. I pictured him on his own on Sunday mornings, happily wheeling compost or dirt or weeds around, wearing thick gardening gloves. He must have loved the day he purchased that wheelbarrow.

I walked onto the steps quietly. There was no way he could hear me. I'd worn sneakers and jeans. The only thing mildly spectacular about my appearance was a brass belt buckle with the silhouettes of two horses. My hair was limp at my shoulders. He'd have to at least level with me if I wasn't dressed like an object.

He opened the door before I knocked. He wore slacks and a dress shirt; the sleeves were rolled up, but he wore a tie. His hair was still buzzed and the skin on his face looked a little rougher, a little dry from shaving. I was looking for things, the shifting. He was beautiful.

"What a great outfit," I said.

"Thanks. I'm technically at work." He looked at me carefully, and I couldn't place myself in his gaze like I used to.

"I recognized your footsteps," he said. We didn't hug each other, though I wanted to and felt a frustrated, capitalist, sense of longing that translated to anger.

"You must love your wheelbarrow," I said.

He stepped out to look around the house. He was barefoot and smelled like perfume. "That's my landlord's."

"Do you ever use it?"

"Maybe eventually—I'm still healing." He rubbed at the corners of his chest. I couldn't help myself—I looked. His shirt was thin and there was nothing to bind him underneath.

"When did all of this start?"

"You know better than to ask that," he said.

"Well, at least some context?"

"Do you want to sit on the swing?" he asked.

I shook my head. "I get nauseous on those."

99

"Let's sit in the doorway." The entry was narrow and it felt strange to have any part of my body pressed up against his. I felt his heat and I wanted him like we had never broken up or undergone ninety days, let alone a year, of no contact. If this was a great experiment, I had failed.

"I got a prescription for hormones the week before we broke up. Took my first shot the night I left. I got this great remote programming job, so I've been able to pay for everything. I had surgery three months ago. Del went with me. A couple folks pitched in. I still have to send thank-you notes."

I rubbed at my eyes like I might cry. I felt a swirl of panic inside me.

"I want to ask why you didn't tell me, but I'm afraid you're going to say that it isn't my business, or that it's not mine to ask about, or some other kind of stoic bullshit." I covered my mouth the way my mother had.

"I'm sorry," he said. "I just needed to make this decision on my own and not discuss the act of making it. Not process it."

"Have you been dating anyone?" I asked. I expected another femme to come walking out of the house wearing an apron, a pie in each hand.

"Yes."

"I can smell her perfume," I said.

He turned his head and looked at me for a long moment, and I wanted to push his face away, but I was afraid to touch him.

"That's mine," he said. "Essential oils. I'm not really into femmes anymore." He gestured to me; it may have been inadvertent, but he still did it. I watched him catch what he'd done. He started playing with the hand that did it.

"I'm more into being with someone masculine, like something equal. It all changed really fast." He reached down and hooked onto his big toes. "I think it's good that you've been dating, though," he said.

"Everyone's been making fun of me."

"They weren't making fun of you exactly. They were testing to see what you knew so they didn't say anything I didn't want them to. They were just trying to be mindful of what I was going through."

"Because you're masculine and worth more than me?" I snapped at him.

"Look at where I'm living. Don't pretend like you don't know what could happen to me. I just don't want anyone else's opinion on how to do this. Sometimes I crave it, but I kind of want to do my own thing and not hear from anyone about what this is supposed to look like, how I'm supposed to act, how other people should act around me. I just want to garden and work this job."

I exhaled and there was a whistle. I coughed and tried to breathe through my mouth.

"You can breathe through your nose. I missed that whistle."

My nose let out a high, sharp whinny, and I wished it hadn't accommodated him like that.

"Are you suddenly nice now?"

"Probably not," he said, and he looked me straight in the eye. "But I'm happier in a lot of ways."

"From the transition or not being with me?" As soon as I said it I wished I hadn't.

"Probably both," he said.

I stood up and walked calmly over to his garden. I looked at the happy, tall plants and rested my hand on one of the tomatoes. I wasn't sure whether to leave or stay, when I felt the plant kind of pulse under my hand. I looked at it and it trembled, probably because my hand was trembling, but I felt this phrase

101

in my brain—*Take me*—and it wasn't coming from me. I felt something like permission when I pulled off the tomato, heavy and green in my hand. I took a bite of it and looked at Dane—he didn't move. I undid the twine from the support and pulled the plant from the ground. The dirt fell away easily, as it had when he pulled this plant from our garden. I laid it down. I pulled out the next plant. And the next. I finished eating the large tomato, and then pulled out a cherry tomato plant and held it up in the air—freshly out of the ground, a sacrifice, its roots dangling. I stared at Dane while I reached for a tomato, plucked it off, and put it in my mouth. The tart acid exploded and I felt my eyes squint, but I didn't stop looking at him. I ate all four of the small tomatoes—each one felt like a bite of power—and then dropped the plant to the ground. Dane still didn't move. I couldn't believe he could sit there like that and not even stand up, not give me any kind of reaction, some sense that he was feeling something.

That was when I undid my buckle and squatted in his garden. I focused my breathing and fixed my eyes somewhere past Dane, who, finally, stood up.

"What the hell are you doing?"

I grunted and grit my teeth. I pushed. Wind whistled out of me. I reached back and spread my cheeks apart, trying to coax out the small pellet I knew was lurking in there. He took long fast steps towards me, but he just looked at me and then my ass, his weight shifting. I could see him measuring whether he should push me over, whether that was a cruel thing to do. I wiggled back and forth and the turd fell to the ground with barely a whisper. It was small and dry. I pulled up my jeans and kicked my legs back, spreading the scent, or covering it with dirt, the way a fox might. My nose whistled. Dane looked into my eyes and I saw that his were brown. It was like I hadn't noticed until

102

that moment because I'd been so focused on what was behind them. Maybe now I saw him seeing me, or maybe I was finally seeing him.

"That wasn't okay," he finally said.

"I know." I finished buckling my belt. "Report me to the queer board of directors. Get me demoted to lesbian."

"The lesbians wouldn't take you," he said. "You shit in people's gardens and wear real fur."

"Only when it's used," I said.

He knelt down and covered the turd with dirt, his hands moving carefully, as if it were a seed. But even planting feels like a burial.

His voice got appropriately soft. "All we had in common was that we liked how wild-looking you could get. It was like dating an animal, and for a while that was perfect because it made me feel like an animal, and what does an animal care about gender? You really performed, and I wanted to do that, too. But I couldn't figure out how to perform and be with you. I didn't want it to be playful. I wanted it to be serious. I think I'm a very serious person and might want a husband and an MBA or something."

A truck turned down the road, the first vehicle since I'd arrived, and crawled slowly past us. The man raised his hand and we raised ours back. He watched us in his rear-view mirror, making sure there was no cause for trouble.

"I know the queer board will vote me out for that," he said.

"More likely the rest of the world will vote you in," I said.

If I hadn't shit in his garden, maybe I would have tried to plead the point that we just hadn't discovered what we had in common, but here we were, on the brink of it. And if he let me live in that house with him, I would make pies all day and he could fuck me at night, when he was done with capitalism, and

103

I'd call him "my man," or I'd wear a suit and buy a dick and show up like a hookup, and we could flip that house together and open up a record shop in a part of town that didn't need a record shop. We could perform gender with such extreme attention to detail that every heterosexual would see us and not feel straight enough, or every gay man from New York would see us and want to buy property here immediately.

But I did shit in his garden, and it revealed some things to me: that I was an animal in his eyes even before that, and that the world would bend away from me even if I wanted to bend towards the world.

So instead, I knelt down, too, and said: "I'm glad you made the decisions you needed to."

He lowered his head and I lowered mine. For this one moment, it appeared as if we were bowed, equally for once, towards each other.

the painting on Bedford Ave.

On August 14, 2003, I decided to put my roommate's painting out on the curb. My girlfriend, Tracy, and I weren't living together, but I was living in an apartment on Bedford Ave. with two of her friends from college. Tracy got me in when my last roommate situation ended horrifically: a bout of bedbugs, a robbery, and my roommate eating all my cream cheese and not fessing up to it. Tracy's ex-girlfriend had finally moved out of the apartment on Bedford and my moving in there meant she would get to hang out with those friends more regularly again. I should have seen that she was dooming me to some kind of pattern of hers, but I was only twenty-four, of middle-class stock, and hadn't yet learned how the system is rigged, or that people have a tendency to fuck up in a specific way, over and over, repeating with varying degrees of severity the same goddamn problem, the same goddamn habit.

I aspired to be a poet and, after a treacherous job search, settled into work at an organic market for most of the week and at a theatre in Flushing, Queens, where I wrote thank-you letters to donors in an office they'd fashioned out of the electrical closet for the other two days. There was one moment when I thought my New York time had come—the world shifting in preparation for something to truly happen—at a party where a former professor introduced me to the poetry editor of the *New Yorker*, one of those not-for-profit-for-life lesbians with lavish hats who, as we shook hands, looked me up and down and said, "I like your handshake."

By the end of the night, she'd given me her card and told me to come in on Monday and she would see about setting me up as a fact-checker. But when I showed up, she wasn't in the office, and though I followed up by email, I never heard from her again.

My roommates, Tamara and Dev, were artists: the former a dancer, the latter a writer and dabbler in oil paints who mostly made a living writing occasional short articles for hip online blogs and established conservative newspapers. Dev's parents very obviously supported her between gigs, so this made it easy to criticize and resent her, especially when, because her bedroom was the smallest, she paid less rent than the rest of us. This didn't add up, as she had taken over a substantial part of the living room as her office. It seemed to me that we should each contribute $583.33, rather than Tamara and I both having to pay $650, but this was the way things were long before I arrived on the scene.

This "new guy" status meant that I was put in the strange centre room that had no windows except for one desperate six-by-twelve-inch slit up near the ceiling that, if I climbed up a ladder, revealed a view of three concrete walls. I got one of those alarm clocks that mimics the sun by slowly getting brighter and brighter as the time to wake up draws near, but all that did was create the appearance that I had slept with the light on, a depressing result that meant I started each day feeling unhinged and like I had no control over my life.

Though I did technically have control over my life then, I was inept at enacting that control and oblivious to all the ways I was supported despite my floundering. And while Tracy, Dev, and I got into deep, self-pitying white-girl conversations questioning what we were supposed to be doing, Tamara never participated or looked moved. She was born in Brooklyn to Haitian immigrants, and her parents weren't into her being a professional dancer. At one dinner, when I asked her what she thought and why she was being so quiet—I'd assumed she was just thinking about other things and wanted to draw her out—she sat up, slung her arm over the back of her chair, and smiled at me the way you do at a baby.

"Who cares what I'm supposed to be doing? I don't have time to think about that. The rest of the world is busy enough trying to make that decision for me anyway. Struggling to be a dancer is the least of my problems," she said. Then her face became more serious, more tired. "Steph, if I'm gonna do this, I have to make it work."

She didn't play the game the rest of us did, where we expressed destitution one moment and bragged about some pipe dream opportunity someone in their thirties promised us that always fell through the next. Instead, Tamara was focused, dancing in a professional company, and always worrying about the potential of suffering some injury, googling phantom pains she felt in

107

the fascias of her feet or in the tendons of her knees. She drank teas that looked like she'd just scooped up the forest floor and used our blender for herbal poultices that gave off a warm, sweet odour when she heated them against whatever part of her body was feeling precarious that week.

—

The night I put the painting outside was so hot—we were in the midst of an unbearable heat wave that threatened to knock out the city's power, and I hadn't been able to sleep at all. I tried all kinds of New Jersey childhood tricks, like putting my pajamas and pillowcases in the freezer. Tamara understood my situation —because she once had the windowless room—and left the small door that connected our rooms ajar and placed her plastic fan in it with the hope that whatever hot air was coming in from her window might make it to my room. It was kind but didn't work.

I tried sleeping in the living room, but Dev had a boyfriend with whom she had effortful-sounding sex, and (from the hum I heard coming from her bedroom but that she denied) an air conditioner, so they could fuck all night long, which made staying on the couch just impossible. I tried to catch her on the air conditioner multiple times, because that meant she should carry more of the electric bill, but I was certain that her boyfriend took the air conditioner in and out of the window frame and hid it in her closet—yes, her bedroom had one of the only closets in that apartment.

Tracy had moved me into the apartment in the fall, when the cool air prompted us to drink dark beer and attempt to make a heating pad sexy. And between these activities, she taught me how to look at Dev's painting.

"Okay, go up close," Tracy said.

I stood in front of the couch, above which the painting hung, my shins hitting the edge of the cushions.

"No, closer," she urged.

I was a new roommate and this wasn't my couch, but because she told me to, I slipped off my shoes and stood on one of the cushions. The painting was a grey-and-yellow checkered pattern with lines that weren't exactly straight. I stared at the squares. Some of the lines waved out slightly, giving me a headache. I looked at Tracy for guidance. Her lip piercing had recently healed, and she compulsively spun the hoop with her tongue, as she had seen every pierced-lip person do before her.

"Now stand back here," she directed.

There was the ghostly form of a man in a suit from the waist up. He looked like a sadly drawn news anchor—the curve of his elbow, the funny oval of his head. I stepped back into Tracy's arms and leaned my face against hers as we stared at the lumpy man in the painting. She rubbed her piercing against the edge of my ear, and I let out a little grunt—felt the heat of her body against my back.

"I know," she said, and kissed my cheek. "It's just so stunning. I knew you would see it. Mega just didn't get it. She thought she was so above everyone."

Mega loomed over our relationship. Mega, who was in her thirties, and a fashion photographer, and not as femme. Tracy was fresh off the breakup when we got together, so in the beginning, all I heard about was the drama, which continued because it took a while for Mega to move out. I was so used to hearing about it that I didn't consider what it meant that I was still hearing about it.

109

"I mean, what kind of person tells an artist to 'hang that fucking piece of shit in your room,' and then within days makes a pass at Tamara, who, I mean, told me and all, and I can't blame her because Mega is so manipulative. I should know. If it weren't for Dev being so hurt by the whole situation, I would probably still be with that snob and missing out on you."

"Well, I love it," I lied, because I was hungry for any opportunity to be a better, more appropriate, girlfriend for Tracy.

Dev walked through the door as we stared at the painting. She had the kind of long commercial hair that she would flip over her shoulder at specific moments, and this was one of them. She smiled and said, "Tracy, I swear, you are, like, my biggest fan."

"Not for long. Soon I'll have competition from Steph here." Tracy held me forward like she was presenting me, and like a puppet, I smiled at Dev.

"You know, you might be right about that having-competition thing." Dev closed the door and came over to us, like she had to whisper some precious secret that would make the rest of New York jealous.

"An assistant from that gallery I was telling you about loved my interview with that female orgasm person in *Nervous Breakdown* and they want me to report on an upcoming show and they said they'd put me in touch with the *Voice*. We're going out for drinks tonight and I suggested they come by the apartment first so I could show them some of my paintings and they are totally in. Can you imagine? If I just got a gallery?"

"Oh, Dev, it's totally going to happen for you. I can feel it," Tracy said.

Dev was always on the verge of some significant break-through. I looked between Dev and the painting and dug my nails into my hand, not to keep myself from saying anything but to be sure that this was all really happening. When Dev went into her room, I closed my eyes and prayed silently: *Please, please, please, don't let that work out.*

Drinks got cancelled, but I was only partially relieved, because I knew, at some point, my prayer would not be answered.

—

On August 14, I was enjoying an unusually quiet afternoon at home. It was my day off and Dev had gone to East Hampton for a long weekend with her boyfriend—one of his friends had gotten a gig house-sitting for Lou Reed and Laurie Anderson and had invited them up to party. I rested on the living room floor, feeling sticky and uncomfortable but better than I did in the furnace of my room. I had my shirt off—Tracy had stayed over the previous night, but our bodies had gotten so hot from wanting each other as much as we did. She went home to Jersey for the day—her parents promised to give her some money for an air conditioner for her bedroom. That morning, we had spoken of it like a great dream.

"I'll buy a cheap one so we can use the rest of the money to take a cab home from Target," she said.

"We'll leave it on all the time," I said, "with the door closed so we can walk into the room and feel relief."

"I'm going to stand in front of it and suck on a Popsicle while you go down on me."

Alone, shirtless, I was contemplating this last scenario when the lock tumbled. It was only one p.m. and Tamara wasn't due back until at least seven. I gasped obnoxiously, which startled her and elicited a similar sound. I moved to put on my shirt, but she just waved a sweating bottle of vodka at me. In her other

111

hand was a small container of orange juice. She limped into the apartment and slammed the door with her foot.

"What happened?" I asked.

Her left foot was bare except for an ACE bandage and she walked carefully on the toes of that foot, letting out little grunts whenever her weight shifted off of it.

"Wanna get drunk with me?" she called from the kitchen.

"I do," I said, with such conviction that I blushed.

She came back with two coffee mugs and a package of frozen peas, which she wrapped around her ankle. Once she was settled, she pressed her face into her hands, let out one sob, then stilled.

"It happened," she said, and moved her foot with the frozen peas forward. The swollen skin was hot, and her ankle was still swelling.

"I twisted it. I knew it was going to be this ankle, too. They told me this was my weak one, and I thought I was doing everything I could, but it was such a simple move. I landed and my foot went one way and my ankle went another way."

"What does this mean?" I asked. The intensity of her grief was contagious and I gave myself over to it.

"My director told me to ice my ankle, and then he gave me this bottle of vodka and told me to drink it. In a few days I might put a hot compress on it, and we'll see. But in the long run, I know this means I'll become a physical therapist or masseuse who used to dance. And if I'm lucky, fucking Dev will be an editor and solicit a review of a dance concert from me for the *Times*, and then she'll reject it."

"What a bitch," I said.

Neither of us had actually spoken ill of Dev before. I stiffened, and the heat covered us. Tamara snorted and filled our mugs with vodka.

"A total fucking bitch," she said.

I splashed orange juice into our mugs, and we swirled it with our fingers and chugged it down because this was like no vodka I had ever tasted. This was how vodka was supposed to taste, kind of smooth and like it was made with vanilla.

"This is a successful New Yorker's vodka," I said.

"It's because my career is over. He would have given me something in a plastic bottle if everything was going to be fine."

I covered Tamara's mouth with my hand, felt the ridge of her teeth meet my skin. "This will heal. We will do whatever it takes to make sure that ankle heals," I said, and though she didn't immediately move her mouth away from my hand, she gave me that look she'd given me before—*You really don't understand anything.*

I refilled our drinks. The vodka warmed me up going down, but I felt myself forgetting the heat.

—

We hit our high, halfway through the bottle, when we stormed into Dev's room, took the air conditioner out of her closet, and jammed it into the window in the living room. We couldn't figure out how to get the window to seal around it, but it didn't matter. We knelt in front of the cold air like it was time for Communion, our tongues extended. At one point, I even started to shiver and crawled away towards our bottle.

The air conditioner made loud chugging sounds, and the power light blinked off and then on again and, finally, in a great scream, off. So did the electricity on the rest of the block. The people of Bedford Ave. shouted, "Hey!" as their air conditioners and TVs silenced. We waited a few moments for the rush of electricity to surge back into our appliances, but there was nothing.

113

Some people were gathering outside, kids running into the street like it was a holiday. Normally, I would have run outside to be part of the commotion, but we were both too disoriented by the headiness of afternoon drunkenness.

We brought the bottle close and leaned against a wall. I talked to Tracy on the phone and worked hard not to sound drunk. NJ Transit trains weren't running back into the city because of the blackout, so she was stuck with her parents. I could tell she was disappointed, and I did my best to comfort her, but I couldn't stop watching Tamara as she created a dance, her beautifully potent leg lifting into the air.

The party outside grew with intensity, a sense of reckless freedom taking hold as the sun began to set and the city, which barely acknowledged the night, descended into an electric darkness. We lit a candle, which caught Dev's painting in a beam of buttery light. The figure was even more apparent, even more grotesque.

"God, I fucking hate that painting!" Tamara shouted. Everyone in the street was shouting now, so it felt good and safe to raise our voices, too.

"This painting," I said. "This painting."

"Say it," Tamara said. "Let it out."

"It fucking sucks. It's the worst fucking painting I've ever seen."

"It makes me fall over," Tamara said. "Sometimes I think of it when I'm dancing and it makes me fall over."

"I was putting mustard on my hot dog the other day," I said, "and I was looking at the colour and the fucking painting came into my mind's eye and I almost threw up. I carried the hot dog for a block and then left it on the ledge of a staircase."

"If you had eaten that hot dog, it would have been like eating the fucking painting."

I sloshed more vodka at Tamara's mug, but some of it missed, landing on the floor and on her leg.

"This painting is a power totem of white mediocrity. Mega said that to Dev one night and I think about it all of the time. This painting. This painting. Ruining our lives," she said.

"I thought she said that Dev should hang it in her fucking room?"

"She also said that. We said a lot about it. And that's where some of its wicked power was, too. Once we started talking about it, we couldn't stop, and then—we just couldn't stop. This painting ruins lives, and Tracy just believes in Dev so much."

"Why doesn't Tracy hang it in her apartment?"

"Mega said that, too. You better watch out. This painting will damn us."

The candle flame trembled and the man in the painting seemed to sway from side to side. Where was he going? I had the urge to lie down, but I knew that once I did, I'd be done for. I made my way up to my feet and took a precarious step forward, felt the top of my body lunge. I took another step.

Here is where my memory becomes faulty. We were both topless. I remember Tamara's face. She was spinning around the room. The painting was in my hands.

"I can dance again," she sang. "You've lifted the curse. I can dance again." Her puffy ankle at work, the thumps from her landings shaking the walls.

I remember my vision trembling and then steadying, trembling and then steadying. I was outside. There was a drum circle on the rooftop next door and another on the street, and they were in counter rhythms, working alongside each other, an offbeat away from merging, but it was coming, as the hands worked skin

115

after skin. The group on the roof gave a hoot when they saw me, and I raised my arms over my head.

"I'm putting it outside!" I shouted at them. "This painting ruins lives." I swayed, felt the painting lift from my hands. "I'm putting it outside."

—

Tamara woke me and I felt that it was impossible that this, the waking up, was happening. I rolled over, the couch groaned, and my neck seemed to respond, too.

"It's almost noon," she said. "There's a strange man sleeping in your bed, the power is still off, and my ankle is worse."

She showed me her ankle, which I will not explain because no part of the human body should look like that. She gave me a shirt and I felt chivalrous as I put it on. I went about my duties with a swollen tongue. I asked the man, who turned out to be our neighbour, and quite friendly, to leave. I wiped up the spilled juice and vodka in the living room, which now felt more capable and lighter, the painting's blank space on the wall like a missing tooth.

Outside, I found there were more people in the street than usual. The painting was propped up against a tree and seemed to be doing no energetic damage there, though maybe it was feeding the commotion around it. The deli on the corner, not wanting their food to spoil, was giving away breakfast sandwiches for a dollar. I got two and a bottle of warm orange juice. There was no ice, but a woman gave me a tube of Icy Hot for Tamara and a bottle of Advil for both of us.

"Tell her to elevate it," the cook said, as he flipped ten eggs in rapid succession. "Drinking might help, too."

116

When I came home, Tamara greeted me like a husband, with a kiss on the cheek. This was the last time in my life that I would ever acquire a best friend with such swift intensity. She extended her hand and I pulled off my sweaty shirt and she hung it on the key rack. We ate our sandwiches topless on the fire escape. We didn't talk about the painting. We used the last of her computer's battery power to watch a movie, snuggled in bed. *This is what it would be like to have one roommate that I liked*, I thought, as she lightly tickled my arm. My hand rested on the thigh of her propped-up leg. The battery was about to die and I was slipping towards sleep.

Then there was a bang, a great hum, and the lights came on. My phone, where it was plugged into the wall, buzzed with Tracy's name, and a kind of roar came from the kitchen and the living room. We stepped out of Tamara's room like the first people, or the last people. The refrigerator was back on and, we discovered in the living room, so was Dev's air conditioner, rattling, cockeyed. Cheers rang out from outside, and there was so much noise that we pulled away from each other. We felt our half-nakedness, the strangeness of our intimacy, the absence of the painting. We put the air conditioner back in Dev's room. I grabbed my shirt off the hook, started to go outside.

"Wait," Tamara said, and suddenly her touch felt different, and my breasts felt different. My phone kept ringing, and I let it.

"Leave it outside, just for tonight," she said. "I'm not ready."

—

Tamara met me after my shift at the market—we knew that our time together was limited. We walked so closely that our

117

forearms met and separated in predictable beats. We needed to bring the painting inside, no matter what state it was in. Dev was asked to cover the aftermath of the blackout for a blog and called Tamara to let her know she would be home sometime that afternoon. Our plan was to confront her about the rent and tell her that we wanted to move the painting to her office area in the living room, or give it to Tracy. If she didn't agree, then Tamara and I would move out, get a two-bedroom in South Slope, or maybe Gowanus. Red Hook was very cheap, and inconvenience then still kept parts of the borough affordable. I pictured us holding hands as we rode bikes over cobblestoned streets.

Just before we reached our building, I grabbed Tamara's hand and pulled her to me. Our bodies rested lightly against each other, except for our faces. In this moment, the city no cooler after the blackout, our lips teased close and pulled away, teased close and pulled away.

The painting kept our lips from touching.

As I gained the courage and moved in with certainty, I heard Tracy's voice. She was holding the painting over her head and she was shaking and I had caused it. I wasn't the first, but I had caused this trembling that would come for her in the wake of each subsequent relationship's end. She fell for someone like this again, and would keep falling, and I would keep hurting someone like this, again and again. And though this time it was the painting's fault, it wouldn't be forever.

Tracy threw the painting with such force it probably would have hit us if it weren't so light. We watched it sail through the air, looking harmless, looking not half-bad, as it landed, miraculously, face up.

seeing
in the dark

When you're a mother there's no point keeping track of the hurtful things your kids say to you. After a while they start to blend together, like the time my daughter told me that the worst part of her day was when she came home from school and I was home too, or that she wasn't gay because I was gay and I repulsed her, or recently, when she told me that she was in a relationship with a woman, but it wasn't part of her identity.

"I'm not like you," she said. "I'm in love."

If she could see how I love her, even though she speaks to me like this.

This child is in her mid-twenties. She's not sixteen.

My friend Barbara once told me that kids get nice again around twenty-four. My baby is twenty-six, and though I'm relieved that she's kind of coming out, finally, I don't see her getting nicer anytime soon. For example, she hadn't been answering her phone, so we set a time for our most recent talk, the one where she said she was in love. When I called her it was loud and she sounded distracted and it turned out she was food shopping. I heard the murmur of her voice as she spoke to someone in the store.

I said, "You want me to call you later?"

And she said, "No, I don't have time later. This is the time we scheduled."

And I wanted to be like, *Yeah, but you aren't listening. You are not in a position to listen, and I know you—if you aren't in a position to listen, which means sitting up on the couch with the TV off and the computer away and looking at me, then you won't take anything in.*

Meanwhile, I had made myself a cup of tea and was sitting at the kitchen table for this call.

My biggest heartache is that this manner of coming out is too late, that she's already done so much damage to herself, that she'll be bitter and mean and closed off for the rest of her life.

But I know this isn't the first time she's been in love with a woman. It's just the first time she's telling me about it.

"Can I meet her?" I asked.

"Where can I find fish sauce?"

"Probably with international groceries," I said.

"I wasn't talking to you," she said.

I pressed my tea mug to my cheek, which was hotter than any tangible feeling between us.

"Well, I'm talking to you," I said. "Can I meet her?"

"I don't know, maybe eventually. There's a picture on Facebook."

"You haven't accepted my friend request."

"Well, I haven't accepted Dad's either. Oh, he's beeping in. Can I call you back?"

—

I used to feel bad for my husband. Privately, in the dark, when I was alone. This experience of feeling bad for him corresponded with missing him. Because I did love him, and I liked sleeping next to his warm, soft body, liked the way we would look at each other when we were laughing, the way he let me cheat at games, the way he always kept my wineglass full during dinner, liked how he knew to get me whisky with Advil when I had cramps, and how he, too, felt joy when they didn't return after Jenna was born.

Yes, I know that all the things I love about him serve me in some way. Jenna has pointed this out time and time again. That's fine if it makes me a bad person, but I think sometimes that's the way love works: one person appreciates the way they are loved, while the other person appreciates the way they get to love. I've been on both sides, so I think I have a fuller understanding. I don't know if Sal will ever experience the other side, which breaks my heart, mostly because it means that he'll never understand me fully and that our reason for splitting is not as simple "we got divorced because she's gay."

He got remarried two years after our split and I'm still single, yet everyone still feels bad for him.

I shouldn't say that. It isn't healing to say that. Anger should be dealt with clearly and directly. This is what I learned from meditation and yoga. I keep up with my spiritual practices because they help me when I wake up at night and I'm staring into the long tunnel of the dark, afraid that the way I see myself is not how the world will ever see me.

121

Sal met a woman on Match.com: Jersey-Italian, too, but fero-ciously straight, defiantly feminine. Her gay husband left her around the same time that Sal asked me for a divorce. She was a high school English teacher, and she said teaching poems to her teenage students helped keep her faith in love alive. She never said this to me. I got it from her Match.com profile as soon as Sal mentioned he was talking to someone on there. The man is so predictable—I knew what he would use for a password (the city he grew up in and the last four digits of his childhood phone number)—and that predictability translated to this woman. She had one child, too, but her body looked younger than mine, and she had a face that cracked with the foundation that covered her smoker's wrinkles. She was still dyeing her hair then, and it was black and curly and long, and she had one of those big-toothed white smiles, and all her pictures were of her in some kind of glittery cocktail dress, except for this one of her on vacation at Long Beach Island wearing a man's sweatshirt and a pair of tight white capri pants with heels.

I knew what their sex would be like: quick and athletic. She's a legs-straight-up-in-the-air kind of woman, and Sal's a woman's-legs-straight-up-in-the-air kind of man. We didn't have sex that way—Sal and I weren't really compatible in bed, and it wasn't because I wanted women more in the end, but because I got bored when he went down on me. Jenna says I'm way too frank about this kind of stuff, and I know she'd be cringing right now.

As far as I know, this woman is the only person Sal dated after our divorce, and he married her. I wasn't invited to their wedding, but once or twice we've had Christmas together—mostly when Jenna was in college, to make her trips home a bit easier—and I can tell that either they have some rare mutual love where they are both the beloved or they are intent on playing at it. They are the kind of people who put up one of those hand-painted signs you can get at flower shops that say "Once Upon a Time" or "They Lived Happily Ever After," with a framed picture of the two of them at a beach house in LBI underneath it.

I haven't experienced love like that, especially since coming out. Sometimes when I'm talking to my older sister, or my cousin for whom the fact that she accepts me is a big deal, I accidentally say things like, "I would never have chosen this path" and "Only straight women know how to value each other."

I say these things and don't know if I believe them.

—

When the phone rang again I picked it up on the first ring.

"I can't talk for much longer," Jenna said. "I just wanted to call you back."

"Has there been anyone else besides—what's her name?"

"Drea," she said. "No. It's not a sexuality thing. We're moving in together once my lease is up."

I heard her car turn on. I stood up and dumped my tea in the sink. The sun was going down and I needed to make sure I wasn't drinking anything with even the tiniest bit of caffeine.

"Are you sure you want to move in with her?"

"It's not like this is just happening," she said. "We've been together for a while. It's just this is the first I'm telling you about it."

"I know," I said. I took a deep breath and made sure to feel my feet on the ground. My anxiety was starting to rise. "But you're just discovering this part of yourself now. Do you really want to be monogamous? Don't you want—"

"Mom. Stop."

"—the opportunity to date other people," I said. "Other women."

I remember when Jenna was a teenager I would talk to other parents about how dating seemed so geared towards monogamy. You didn't go out on dates—you asked someone to go out with you, like be monogamous with you right away, and there was no room to really decide if you even liked being around the person first. This is probably my generation's fault, having something to do with the accessibility of sex. But I don't know what I'm talking about. Yes, Sal asked me out on dates in high school, and there was another boy or two that I was going on dates with, but I wasn't having sex with all of them, or even making out with them all. I ended up only really making out with Sal, and then only having sex with Sal.

Jenna was so adamant. She was in love, and they were moving in together.

"I waited to tell you until I knew we were going to be serious." She was exasperated. I heard her breathing change the way it does before she cries. "I didn't even want to tell you—"

"Jenna, you're not breathing. Calm down—"

"—because I knew you were going to make this about you!" she screamed.

I felt her voice slice into my heart. The wound children make there? It never heals.

Finally, her voice calmed. "I'm not like you. I'm in love."

—

I saw a picture of the two of them on Facebook: Drea is this really tall butch in a pinstriped suit who I wouldn't have been able to tell was a woman right away, and I wondered if she even thought of herself as one. I prefer women who look like me, I guess. Jenna looked more feminine than ever sitting on Drea's lap with her arms wrapped around her neck, and that made my heart so happy because I felt like maybe everything was going to be okay. Jenna was finally coming into herself.

I saved the picture on my computer. I want Jenna to remember, or even notice, that she looked like that, full and available. From an energetic standpoint, I could see that all her chakras were open and spiralling into the universe, which I'd never seen in her before, at least not around me.

There's a picture of myself that I love.

It was taken six months before the divorce. This was after I came out, when I had the romance with Tina, and Sal knew about her, we'd even all had dinner together. There was this one day when we all went to Jenna's baseball game and I sat between my husband and my lover. The assistant coach was taking pictures of family members and he snapped one of the three of us. My arms are around both of them, and my smile is open and big. My hair looks good, too. Tina and Sal look happy and at ease. I look at that picture and try to come up with a different narrative—not that we are all together in one relationship, but that I am able to be with both of them, and we all respect and love each other. In this narrative I even imagine Sal's wife somewhere in the background, waiting for him to meet her for a date after. Maybe she and I go to the movies. I'm not looking for a threesome—it just would have been nice if that day at the baseball diamond, the way I felt, the moment that was captured, could have been real.

I barely date anymore. An astrologer in my women's healing circle told me that there was a planetoid blocking Venus and it would take a few years for that to clear. She also said, "There isn't one committed partner in your future," looking sad when she told me, remorseful, like maybe she should have kept it a secret. I felt sad when I heard it, too, and that evening, as we made these chakra bowls ring out, I mourned that prophecy, and longed for Sal again. That feeling of partnership.

I've been trying to rethink what the astrologer told me. Maybe by one committed partner she just meant that I wasn't going to get everything from one person, the way that Sal and his wife seem to.

I think that's what I wish I could warn Jenna about.

But maybe Jenna and Drea have that mutual kind of love. Maybe they have what Jenna and I once had, when she was a baby and I was her everything.

Late at night, I feel like there was some opportunity, some other way to be, and I missed it. It's dark and I'm squinting down this long, spiralling tunnel, and I know there is something more out there than just wanting to sleep with women, something close to what exists in that picture, but I can't quite see it.

the wallaby

My farmer neighbour asked me if I wanted to meet his wallaby. That summer, I'd moved to the land adjacent to his property and was working all day and into the night to get a sixteen-foot flatbed shipping container ready for me to live in by the fall. When I first started the work, I didn't realize that some systems—the water main, the electrical grid—are just waiting for you. That you're often building just to reach what's already there. Not totally unlike when I got married—even though I didn't believe in marriage; even though I ran away to the city to live with my sister in a community that was supposed to disrupt supremacist and normative thinking; even though, or maybe because, as an adult I spent my time submitting grant reports to foundations—because I still fell in love hard, and I wanted to marry her, couldn't think of anything but marrying her, and having bookshelves and matching plates and a nice apartment together. It wasn't until I moved to this land and plugged plumbing into the earth that I understood that my idea of love had tapped into the systems that were already waiting for me.

My sister, Stacy, and I had bought these two acres of land outside Seattle from the farmer years before, with the intention of making it a retreat for activists, but retreat as in actual retreat. We went out there to camp and cook vegan food over a fire with the rule that we couldn't talk about anything important, but because we were 501(c)3 addicts we talked compulsively about all the things we could turn this land into, like a camp for trans and queer youth. We thought we had time.

"I want to die out there," she told me.

"You can't die outside," I replied. I wasn't sure how to orchestrate that, how to keep her comfortable on rough land. And even though the Pacific Northwest weather was typically beautiful and predictable in the summer, it just seemed too cold a place to die. We had this conversation on a loop.

"Who's to say I can't die outside?"

My sister never listened to me, but in this one thing I had what felt like the world's agreement, and I ran with the conviction of the doctors' conclusion that she was not thinking clearly. Doctors would say things about how it seems good to die out in nature until you are actually dying and you are in pain and it's already so hard. One nurse told me sternly, "Everything should be as comfortable as possible."

Our final conversation about it was at a lounge in Chelsea that had once been our favourite muffin shop—a previous gentrification outdone. We went there mostly as a joke, but when she ordered a hot toddy I got mad and told her to take it back, and she said, "You can't tell me what the fuck I can do. You can't tell me where I can die."

"You told me what the fuck I could do."

"That's because you were a baby."

"Well, now you're dying." Though she said it plenty, I had never said it before.

She pulled her drink close and the steam curled up around her chin, which looked weird because it was late May and everyone, except for Stacy, was in T-shirts. She was wearing thermals, and two sweaters. I'd helped her dress that morning.

"Remember when you told me I couldn't fuck your roommates and then I kissed Jill?"

"You didn't kiss Jill! I don't remember that."

"I told you the next day." I felt an old discomfort rise in me but tried to ignore it.

"If that happened, I would have made us move. It seems like a good idea to kiss someone, but then you can't stop kissing them."

"It seems like a good idea to die in nature," I told her, "until you are in pain and it's already so hard."

"It's gonna be messy anywhere. Why is there a rule that I need to die inside?"

"You told me sex was messy and you needed us to be comfortable. This is about being comfortable."

"Who cares about being comfortable?" she said a little loud for a lounge like this. I felt embarrassed, even though no one looked at us. "I'm already uncomfortable. This is about dying where I want to die."

"How am I gonna take care of you out there?"

And maybe underneath that she finally heard the subtext of my words: *How do I explain your body when you go, and what do I do with it after, and what happens when you move your bowels, and can't someone else just take care of all that?* Our eyes held each other's gaze, and maybe my eyes were doing what hers once did to me when I was sixteen—agreed with me, lied to me, so we could pretend everything was okay. She heard all of this without my needing to say it and gave me the familiar look of compassion and disappointment that older siblings are so good at. She sipped her drink and didn't say, *Fine*, but I heard her anyway.

She looked like her flamboyant self until the beginning of June, when she was on hospice in me and my partner's apartment. The Brooklyn summer was blazing outside and she was inside and pale and nothing would make her comfortable, and when her breath was grinding through her body, all I could think about was that land and how her time in her body should be ending there. I knew that after she was cremated I would spread some of her ashes there, but once I spread them I didn't see how I could ever leave her, how I could ever come back to New York without her.

—

When the farmer asked me if I wanted to meet his wallaby—and I was certain this wasn't a euphemism—I got a bit friendlier.

"How many wallabies you got?" I asked. "You, like, milk them?"

"That's not what you keep them for!" the farmer said, laughing. "Their teats are in the pouch. Can you imagine reaching your hand in there and milking that? You'd have to get the tiniest bowl of milk of all time."

He pantomimed pulling a pouch back on himself and reaching a hand in, and someone driving by might have thought he was hitting on me. He must have realized the same thing because his hand went rigidly to his side.

130

"I only got one," he said. "Named Dandy. But I'm thinking of getting a female. You sell the babies for a grand. And they're always making them, too. In the bush, they have one in the pouch and one waiting up inside. If a dingo chases them, they just throw out the one in the pouch so the dingo will leave them be, and then the next one will crawl out and into the pouch. Come on."

He opened his gate and motioned for me in that male way where it's clear there isn't much of a choice.

The farmer had beautiful land, just about ten acres in high harvest, and it gave me a sense of the potential of my blackberry-overrun property. Three farmhands were finishing up for the next day's market. They waved vitally, then went back to washing the last of the salad mix.

The farmer asked me to help him move a tarp of compost back to its covering. He pointed out his cows, sweetly munching in a field beyond, and then his house, where the chickens ran like something out of a storybook. A field of calendula, a thicket of wild rose, and then a fence with a sweet purple gate led us into the wallaby run.

Dandy stood there, a small grey wallaby, with his giant feet and his tiny, weird black-leather hands. He was smaller than I expected, but he stretched his length a bit and exposed a long, wiry, pink penis.

The farmer laughed. "Put that situation away, Dandy." He chuckled again in my direction, feigning embarrassment. "Poor thing," he said.

Dandy had beautiful long black lashes that disappeared when he got excited, his eyes large.

"Now," said the farmer, "he likes people and you can pet him, but we got him when he was mature, out of the mom's sack, and

131

they aren't as sociable once they're out. I breed them, I'll have to sell them to people when they're still in a pouch so that way they can bond."

"The mom's pouch?" I asked.

"No, it's like—" and Dandy was on him, grabbing the farmer's hands with his little weird ones and gnawing a finger sweetly with his white buckteeth. The farmer petted his head and then pried the tiny hands off his.

"Don't let him grab you," he said. "I'm trying to train him out of that. He's sweet but a little persnickety. They're love bugs when you get one still in the pouch."

Dandy came over and nibbled at the bottom of my shirt. I pet the top of his head—standard fuzzy, maybe like petting a rabbit. He went to grab at my hand and I pulled it away. I didn't understand why the farmer would want to train him from grabbing a hand, but I also didn't feel like asking. I'd seen the wallaby and now I wanted to get back to work.

"I should probably get him a female. It's not right, him being alone out here."

"What does he eat?" I asked.

"Exotic pet food," he said. The farmer motioned and, as if on cue, Dandy hopped over to his feed area. Every time he moved it was like he'd never moved before. I couldn't tell if that was because he'd never been outside the narrowness of the run, or if this was a strangeness particular to the wallaby anatomy. Before I left the farmer showed me the pouches he was already knitting for the wallabies to come, spools of red and blue wool cluttering his dining room table.

That night, I watched videos of wallabies in the wild, of a baby poking its head out of the pouch. In a dream, someone reached

132

down my pants, found a teat, and stroked it for milk. I woke up thinking of Dandy, alone, waiting behind that purple gate.

—

While Stacy's breath was still rattling I knew my partner and I would split. We'd discussed it even before our apartment became a literal place of dying. Significant breakups were familiar to both of us, but we didn't understand how much uglier it would feel having to get an actual divorce. When marriage had become legal we'd gone to city hall, subversively wearing chaps and sparkly underwear. We had strangers—two silver foxes—be our witnesses because I knew my sister wouldn't be into it. Not that she wasn't happy, or didn't think it was useful that marriage was legal, but when we told her afterwards, a bit giddy, she just said, "Now you get to have the law involved if you want to break up."

After she died, I took what I inherited from her life insurance, left my job, headed west, like European invaders do, and started building where a house had once stood and then burned down, which was why I could so easily plug in most of the modern conveniences.

By November, my little home was set up and cozy. I'd built a composting toilet a few feet away and constructed a kind of bath shack with a tub inside and a shower outside. When the blackberries died back, I attacked them with a machete.

The farmer stopped by one day and offered to help with his farmhands. I asked about Dandy and he said that he was about to be doing much better. They had just gotten a pet goose to live in the run with him, and they'd gotten a dog about his size and they'd really taken to each other.

"They love to box; you should see them. Really shows how small a wallaby's brain is when a dog gets tired of playing with him. Same thing over and over. But, man, it's cute."

After a few hours of work, two of the farmhands took off—they were just doing a favour, after all—but one of them stayed. She was at least twenty years younger than me, with a nose ring and a cute short haircut covered by a bandana. She was just the type of girl I went for again and again, and I felt like a time capsule: older body but same desire. She was giving me these little looks that indicated she didn't care about my age, and I might have given her a look that meant the same thing. I think the farmer was waiting for her to want to quit, so he stayed and helped way longer than he intended. Around dinnertime he stretched, picked at some splinters in his thumb, and said he'd better head in and rest. The farmhand asked me if I was going to work for a little longer.

"Just a bit," I said. "But I got it from here."

"I'm not tired and could still help, if you don't mind. I'd love to see how you set that container up."

I said that would be fine and the farmer left us. As soon as he walked away, she put her shears down and stretched her arms up over her head.

"I'm a yoga teacher," she said.

"That's good," I said, swinging at a blackberry vine. "I'm sure the other farmhands like that."

"Yeah. I could give you a private session, if you like."

"It's okay," I said. "I don't like yoga."

Her eyes got wide like the wallaby's, but her lashes didn't mysteriously disappear—still long and black and kind of extravagant, like they were covered in grease.

134

"I bet you just haven't had the right teacher," she said.

"No," I said. "Sometimes people just aren't into things."

I picked up her tool and motioned for her in a way I thought was gentle, not like the farmer, but the way she followed reminded me that I was masculine. We took our shoes off outside the container. She ran her hand along the metal ridges, and when I opened the door, she crossed in front of me.

"So cool!" she cooed.

The container had once been used for trekking frozen things across the country, so it was insulated. A bed was at one end and I'd put a window by the oven, which let in a nice amount of light. I lit the stove and put the kettle on. The farmhand took pictures of the space with her phone.

"Are you gonna live in this place forever?" she asked.

"I might."

"There's enough room for another person, I guess," she said.

"I'm not worried about that."

She looked down at her hands. I could tell she was trying something with me she'd never tried before, and I felt bad for her.

"Would you like to see the bathhouse?" I asked.

"Cool," she said.

I took her out back and she oohed and aahed, and I suggested she take a bath. "You did all that work for me. Least I could do. I'll make you some food, too."

I know I offered these things, but I didn't exactly expect her to say yes. I just didn't want her to feel bad. It doesn't take long being around a twenty-year-old before I start thinking like one.

While I cooked, I heard her singing from the tub—it was the kind of night that carried sound lucidly, and I bet the farmer, or at least the other farmhands, could hear her. I cut up vegetables that she'd probably pulled from the ground and washed. I thought about how nice it would be next year when I would be

135

able to use at least some of my own food. It's a bit obscene when you think of it, eating the food that other people grow rather than what you make happen.

It was too cloudy for stars and her singing ceased and the night carried the energy of her wanting me to come out and check on her. It rushed electrically between the bathhouse and the container. I figured she was wondering how that works and I knew I could show her how it works, the way Jill showed me. I knew what role was there for me.

—

Once, when I was eighteen, I was asked to speak at a fundraiser for the youth program Stacy had set me up with after I ran away. She went thrifting for weeks to find a suit that our roommate Jill could tailor, and it felt like the best thing I'd ever worn, not just since running away but like the best outfit I could possibly put on my body. But when I got to the ballroom, because of either the lighting or the crisp shininess of all those rich people's clothes, my suit looked drab and strange and didn't actually fit me as well as I thought. Even though I would have hated it, I felt like I should have worn a dress. Bill Cunningham took photos and I wasn't in the spread for the *Times*, which wasn't even what bothered me. The organization had also invited my friend Marquis to speak, the only Black person present. During the cocktail hour, I watched as they ignored him or, like, touched him too much, making a fuss over his suit, white hands constantly on his shoulders. I think I felt that pull from the world we were getting money from—that all it would take was for me to grow my hair long and wear a dress and it could take me in.

"Let it make you angry," Stacy said that night. "All these systems are waiting right underneath you, and if you aren't paying attention, you become complicit."

That night, I really took in those tennis bracelets that caught the light, and the men with their grey hair and younger wives, and the number of empty champagne bottles Marquis and I counted when we snuck into the caterer's area to hide. When the auction started, paddles were getting raised for $5,000, $15,000. I remember watching one table where a woman bid something like $5,000 for a weekend vacation, and when she couldn't go up any higher, a man at her table lifted his paddle again and again, until, at $12,000, he won the vacation and gave it to her. She said thank you like he'd bought her a coffee or something, and he said, "Not a problem" like he'd just taken out the trash.

Marquis and I laughed, but then he looked at me half-surprised but mostly amused. "These are your people," he said.

"They aren't."

"No, for real, they are."

—

I married. I got an apartment in a gentrifying neighbourhood and didn't become part of the community. I set up fundraisers to keep rich white donors comfortable and happy and blind to their complicity.

Now I was on a farm, and maybe it looked like I was doing something different, but I was on this farmer's land, not a farmer, with a farmhand waiting in a tub for me. I don't know what we can ever have control over, when the wiring is there and my sister is not.

137

I was chopping beets when the farmhand came chirping in, clean and shiny in her filthy farm clothes.

"You cry from chopping beets?" she asked.

"All the time," I said. "You need another shirt?"

"Sure." She sat down at the table. "That's my favourite thing about cleaning up after a day like today, putting on a clean shirt."

"Big pleasures," I said, "out here on the farm."

She blushed. I gave her a shirt that was particularly warm and soft, and we turned away from each other while she changed.

She warmed her hands on a mug of tea. I put the vegetables in a pan to cook and told her I was going to take a quick shower, and if she didn't mind swirling them from time to time, that would be great. The water was hot and the air was cold. I think in books, older people's bodies feel younger when they are about to get with a person with a younger body, and though I felt that option waiting for me, I chose instead to just feel older.

I put on a clean shirt and when I went inside dinner was done and she'd set out two dishes. We ate and the feeling settled over me—like it always does before I fuck someone I'm going to fall in love with—that I already knew the farmhand. And maybe because I'm older I did know a version of her, I'd dated her before, I'd confused and hurt her before. I enjoyed the feeling of eating in the kind of silence that comes from already loving someone for years.

We didn't sleep together that first night. She just didn't go home, and neither of us slept. We sat at the table for so long that my body began to ache from the chair, and then for even longer we sat on the floor, with our backs against the wall. Do I remember the moment we moved towards the bed? No. But she just sat at the edge of it, and then near dawn I started to doze, still sitting upright. I heard the rooster from the farm and got up to make her coffee. I had that chill that overruns the body after a sleepless night, the feeling of impending diarrhea. I could go to bed—I could slack off on my land for at least one more day—but the farmhand didn't have that option. And maybe it was just to make it all worth it, but she came forward and kissed me. Her lips were chapped and cold, and she tasted like the garlic from last night's dinner and the coffee I'd just made her.

"Can I come back when it's time to sleep?" she asked.

All these systems are waiting right underneath you, and if you aren't paying attention, you become complicit.

"Yes," I said.

—

When the farmhand came back that evening she shared the big drama that had occurred on the farm: a raccoon had gotten into the wallaby and goose run and killed the goose, totally severed its head from its body. I thought of Dandy watching this—did wallabies have any ability to help? They found Dandy with a gouge out of his neck but okay, just hopping nervously. I thought of Dandy looking at his tiny hands, and the raccoon's tiny hands, and maybe for a moment he found himself and reached for the raccoon's head.

The farmhand, trying to describe the sharp, desperate chittering sound, the stress sound that Dandy made, began imitating it in sharp, high gasps. I wanted it to stop, so my mouth found her mouth, her belly, her cunt, like a tiny sum of nickels. After she came, with my fingers worked their way inside—three, then four, then five, my hand closing into a fist, only my wrist outside her—she gasped and attempted to look like this had happened for her every time. I thought of the woman who was once older

139

than me, who first put my finger in her so that I asked if this was sex, and I looked at the farmhand now and wondered if this was sex. I wanted my sister to see what Jill had done. I wanted to know whether it was sex. The younger woman's hands ran along the inside of my thighs, then out and around my ass, but my body was numb, like always. Her hands were there, but I didn't feel them. Her body shook and she made moans that sounded like gibberish and became real speech.

"Your skin's seen a lot," she said.

"Like what?" I asked, hoping she would see what Jill had done to me, my sister's complicity.

"Resistance," she groaned. "History."

—

She left for the farm early. What was I even doing on mine? I hauled the torn-up blackberries away. I sowed cover crop on my one measly row and borrowed the farmer's tiller. When I returned it, he looked at me like I had been messing with his stuff.

"How's Dandy doing?" I asked, interested in getting him to stop trying to figure out how the sex worked.

"Healing. Wanna see him?"

I didn't, but I nodded. We went beyond the wild rose, back to that purple gate. And there was Dandy, standing tall like last time, with a pink of exposed flesh, only now it was on his neck. The farmer picked him up by his mighty tail so I could get a closer look, and Dandy's little arms writhed. The wallaby grabbed my hand and I let him chew on it.

"Don't let him do that," the farmer said.

I didn't move my hand. I let him move Dandy from me instead.

"I put an order in for a female. She'll still be in a pouch when she gets here, but it feels like the least I can do. You wouldn't want to help, would you? Once she's matured and mating and birthing?"

I hesitated and the farmer spoke a bit faster.

"We could do a trade. I could give you a farmhand for a few hours. I know you two've hit it off."

I told him I'd think about it.

"I'll need help to arrange all those sales. Once we're making money, I could pay you. Doesn't look like you got big plans for your land anyway, and money probably wouldn't hurt."

But then he sort of sneered, at least, I saw it as a sneer.

"Maybe, though, money's not something you need."

—

I walked home and looked at my three prepped beds. I was hoping to put in some drip irrigation but mostly wanted to leave it all alone. I didn't want to have big plans for the land. Even that one field seemed like an exposure.

That night in bed the farmhand looked excited. She mentioned what the farmer had said. She was excited for Dandy.

"I'm not," I said.

"You want him to stay alone?"

"No. But it's better than creating more babies that have to go off and be alone somewhere else.

"It's good money," she said.

I started feeling cold, so I pulled my shirt on. I got up and found a stale package of cigarettes I had saved from New York. While Stacy was in hospice I took up smoking to have an excuse to go outside. I lit one and frowned. It tasted like Stacy was dying.

"She won't be birthing until just as I'm finishing. I could stay here and help you out," the farmhand said.

"You can take the baby out of the pouch?"

"No, I can put the baby in the travel pouch in which it will arrive ready to love its new owners." When I didn't say anything she stood up, too, took a stale cigarette, but when she heard the sound of it crackle, she didn't light it, just held it in her hand. "I could help you really turn this land into something. You have a fair amount of space here."

"I really don't want to turn this into anything."

It's likely that I motioned towards her. She flicked her unlit cigarette at my chest.

"You think you can be a guy by acting like a guy?"

"No," I said. I put out my cigarette in the sink. "I think I can be alone by acting like I want to be alone."

"You could have other queers here in shipping containers. You could really transform this community."

I thought of the plans Stacy and I used to talk about and replaced them with all these adult white queers in shipping containers, seeming much nicer when you get them still in the container than when you get them without the container.

"It's a nice night," I said. "Can I walk you home?"

If she were older, she might have told me to fuck off and walked herself home, but instead, she nodded and we walked quietly to her little shack—a trendy thing to get to live in when you don't grow up in poverty. If you get them to go willingly into the shack, they're less persnickety. We hugged good night and I held her close, even though her body tried to squirm away.

I headed over to Dandy. Inside his run I turned my headlamp off and he bounced over. Soon, he wouldn't be alone and he'd settle into a nice monogamy—what does Dandy care if the

142

babies go? He grabbed and bit at my hands, tentatively at first, and when I didn't jerk away, he became more aggressive, more joyous. I did too, giving him pressure, giving him resistance. I wasn't numb. I felt his fur against me, his teeth in my skin.

the only
pain you feel

"Stormy night tonight," my father said.

We were seated at the card table—the one flat surface in his new one-bedroom apartment. He was the one who asked for the divorce, but with good reason: my mom was gay. And though she was content to stay married and carry on her affairs, as she had done for years, he was not.

"Stormy," he said again.

I couldn't speak, and the divorce wasn't the reason. There were two—one was fairly practical, but the other was conceptual and beyond my father's realm of easy understanding. I was sixteen and had started my period a month ago. That inaugural period had a strange thrill: my father bought me flowers when he found out, and my mother gave me a light smack on the cheek with the blessing *May this be the only pain you feel as a woman*, which, looking back, was a joke because I was cursed with a new kind of pain that rages through my body and leaves me dry-heaving in more dramatic moments and curled up shivering in more subtle ones. This is a kind of inheritance from my mother's family.

"All the women on my side have it," she said. She was wrapped in a series of robes, on her way out to a kirtan at the yoga studio she attended.

"Once you have a baby, it goes away. Finish packing for your father's. I'm off to sing for the Lord!"

Now my father looked at me, nudged my plate of chicken nuggets closer.

"I have cramps," I told him.

He reached over and took a bottle of ibuprofen from the silverware drawer, a strange place to keep it, but this was his home and he had a right to store things wherever he pleased.

"You get them like your mother?"

I nodded. He led me to the couch and with the pills gave me a cup of instant cocoa spiked with whisky.

"I don't know if whisky fits into your mom's lifestyle now, but it was the only thing that did the trick until she had you."

My cramps weren't as bad as they could be, but I wanted my dad to feel useful, and in fact, the whisky did me good for the second reason I felt unable to say. In the bathroom, where the wind shook the windowpane so hard I thought it might shatter towards me, I looked down at the pad, and in addition to the dried blood—I was not yet fastidious enough at changing this strange diaper—there was a layer of fresh, orange blood. A clot dropped into the toilet. Staring at both the blood that spread in the water and the evidence in my pad, I was struck: this blood belonged to me, and it would come out like this with the purpose of being discarded every month. It seemed like one should make

146

use of it, like donate it or save it for when you needed it later. The female body was so wasteful—at least mine was—waiting for something that might never happen.

That was the actual reason. I realized that I might be in love, and I did not want my father to think I was anything like my mother.

—

She was two years older than me and I met her in an upstairs bookstore in a part of Asbury Park that was getting turned around, which meant that white gay men were moving into a predominately Black community and soon the rent would go up. I didn't know it then, but she was watching me from the women's studies section. When I glanced up, I thought she was a boy. This worked to both our advantages because if I had thought of her as a girl from the outset, I wouldn't have been caught off guard and learned anything about myself.

"Look," she said.

I looked into her face—which was tiny, even her ears were small—and I think it was at her mouth where I got confused, because her lips were soft and available despite the sharp line of her jaw, a physical attribute that will always mean handsome. She had a kind of Elvis do: her hair was thick and black, but in the glow of the fluorescent lights it looked almost navy. She narrowed her eyes at me, and then she realized that I was staring at her so intently because she'd told me to.

"No. Look behind you. It's the Boss."

I turned to see Springsteen, looking like he'd just walked out of a magazine, leaning against the counter and speaking with the bookstore owner. Though he was often sighted around town, 147 especially since all the changes that had been taking place, it was strange to see him on the customer side of the counter. He was not meant to be an ordinary man. His eyes glanced over at me, not to see me but to keep watch over himself. I felt chastised because a real Shore girl knows that *he is a man*, just one that belongs to us.

I turned back to Jess—who I didn't know was Jess yet—and she gave me a knowing smile, then returned to her book. I went into her aisle and flipped a book open, just so I could stand next to her. I didn't read the title, so I was surprised to open to a picture of one woman holding a mirror up to another woman's vagina. I turned the page quickly, nearly tearing it, and looked over at Jess to make sure she hadn't seen. But she was looking at me now, and she had seen.

"I'm Jess," she whispered.

The Boss might have been a man, but he was still the Boss, and it didn't seem right to speak too loudly in his presence.

"I've been here when he's come in before. He loves Steinbeck. They're always negotiating for some first edition somewhere."

"Wouldn't he have them all by now?" I asked.

"There's more to books than being a first edition that make them special. He wouldn't want just any first edition. He'd want the one that belonged to Steinbeck's sister, or maybe an ex-lover who was also an ex-writer."

Jess turned back to her book and the cover flashed at me. It was silver with hot-pink lettering.

"My mom got me that book here. It's signed."

She grunted.

"Mine must be a newer edition or something," I said. "It doesn't have a cover like that. I tried to read it, but it seemed kind of whiny and gay."

Bruce stepped into another room, so even though her voice could return to normal, Jess kept a tight rein on it.

"You mean, like stupid or like it's about gay people?"

She's gay, I thought, and looked down. I shrugged. I was sixteen, so I used my sixteenness to get out of it.

"My mom is gay," I said. "Like actually gay."

"I am too," she said. She closed the book and moved away to buy it.

"I can give you my copy," I said.

"Don't give away what your mom gave you. It's signed and you might want to read it now. Anyway, this is for a friend."

What did that mean, I might want to read it now? I wondered what kind of friend. I followed her to the counter. The owner seemed unmoved by Springsteen's visit and I resented him for it, that he was able to be more advanced so as to not be affected by him.

"I have that book," she said, motioning to the one with the picture of the giant vagina, still in my hands. "Great purchase."

Before I could say anything, the owner snatched it and rang it up. It wasn't expensive, I had enough for it, but I felt like I had done a terrible thing—my dad said it was dangerous to spend money when you didn't intend to. Jess didn't need a bag, but I took one, and we walked down the flights of stairs together.

"You had a coffee at the renovated Howard Johnson's yet? All the new artists in town hang out there."

I shook my head.

"Let me take you," she said.

Even though I was with someone, and even though a white guy in tight orange pants shuffled past us, I wasn't certain we were supposed to be walking in this part of town. My parents always ran red lights here and the cops had never pulled them over for it.

149

"They have more important things to take care of," my dad said each time we cruised through a light and past a police car's passionless grille.

Once we passed the initial row of new shops, we hit a long stretch of abandoned, crumbling buildings extending all the way to the beach. Up ahead at the corner, two Black men in construction clothes and boots were in conversation. The shorter man had his hard hat on and was using his work gloves to imitate someone talking, and the other man, who had his hat off, was taller, even though he stooped, his arms wrapped around his middle, laughing, until he saw us.

"Lost?" he asked.

I looked down.

"Nah, we're just up ahead," Jess said.

I was surprised that she spoke, that she didn't apologize, that she didn't sound nervous. I stole a look at Jess, whose boyishness I thought glowed with vulnerability as she moved to walk around them, but the taller man took a large exaggerated step to the side.

"Pardon me," he said.

I looked up and nodded, and he didn't nod back. He wore wire-frame glasses, the arms wrapped around his ears. His face was set still and communicating something, but no one had ever told me that I should try to read it, so I didn't. I looked down again, a direction I'd come into the world to look, and didn't raise my eyes until we reached the boardwalk.

We got a seat by the window. The Atlantic crashed plaintively on the sand where I'd once found a pen shaped like a hypodermic needle. My mom screamed as she slapped it out of my hand. She gave no explanation when we started going to the beach at Avon, where mostly everyone was white and visibly sunburned, just like the customers standing around in the Howard Johnson's. I ordered what Jess ordered: a latte, and the hot milk mixed with the bitter coffee was a kind of revelation.

"How old are you?" I asked. I liked the way she held her cup in front of her face at all times, and I tried to imitate that look without seeming like I was imitating her at all.

"Eighteen," she said, and I couldn't help it, I smiled real big. My mom told me there was a world of difference between my age and eighteen, but two years wasn't too old. For what? I asked myself.

She looked nervous. "Why, how old are you?"

"Sixteen."

"I thought you were older," she said, and I knew I should have lied.

"I bought that book you got today when I was sixteen. It was really important for me getting to know my body and stuff." She blushed, and then I did, too. "So your mom's gay. Did she come out later?"

"Yeah, my parents are divorced. My dad is pretty sad."

She nodded, and I memorized the way she took a sip of her coffee, thoughtfully, as if the next phrase was hidden in the liquid suspended in her mouth.

"He won't be for long. He'll end up just fine."

"You don't know that. He's really sad."

"You doing okay with it?"

I shrugged, and then remembering that she was gay, I became concerned that she would interpret it wrong. So I tried out taking a thoughtful sip of my coffee, but it was just cold and bitter now and lacking whatever inspiration it might have once held.

"I worry about them. My mom has all these new hobbies and has gone through two breakups already that she took really hard. Actually, can I run something by you?"

She nodded, but now, I can see that she didn't want me to.

"She took the first breakup a lot harder than she took the divorce with my dad, and she told me that's because the intensity of time is different, so for example, if you are in a relationship with a woman for a year it equals four years with a man. Is that how it is?"

"Hoo!" Her face turned red and she gasped for breath, and then again, "Hoo! Hoo!"

Soon I realized that this sound was her laughter. *Hoo! Hoo! Hoo!* It was so loud and so resonant that the artists looked at us, and I wondered, when they looked at me, across from her, whether they thought I was gay, too.

"That's like, I'm sorry, but I feel like from now on I'm going to ask people how long they've been together in gay years."

"It isn't true?"

Jess wiped her eyes and the hoos restrained within her sent her body into rhythmic shakes.

"Well, I've never been with a man but—"

"You haven't?" I asked, and then covered my mouth.

"Have you?" she asked sharply.

I shook my head.

"Well, there's hope for you yet." She was no longer in a laughing mood. She ran her hands through her hair and I watched the pouf wilt flat, like a mood indicator.

"I think there is a different kind of intensity, but that's just a result of oppression. It's weird to be a community when all you have in common is how you feel about gender and who you want to have sex with. But you need it—I need it. I know that whenever I've fallen in love, I knew it the first time we slept together. Plus, there are no rules telling you to play any kind of game, no rule that you have to meet each other's parents first, or

152

wait a year to move in together. With my first girlfriend, after the first night, I never went home again."

I wondered if she'd had many girlfriends, and I felt jealous of the person who was going to get that book.

"I just don't want to ever be sad the way that my dad is sad, and I don't want to ever do things the way my mom did them," I said.

Jess's face softened and I saw what my mom meant, about the difference between sixteen and eighteen: you still knew something about the pain of parents, but you were starting to be free of them.

"Most likely you won't," she said. "They already did all of that for you."

At my dad's house, I lay on the couch in some pain, mildly drunk, thinking about that conversation and how I already knew then that I was in love with her.

—

Before my mom came out, she was always asking me if I was gay. Sometimes she wouldn't ask, she would just say so, especially on the phone to strangers I would later figure were my mom's secret lovers.

"I don't know. Jenna just doesn't seem to like boys."

The asking started early, in elementary school: "Got any little boyfriends, girlfriends?" Always with a nervous laugh.

I thought it was my fault, because of the time I was four and tried to kiss her like they do on TV, and she let me, my tongue slipping into her mouth, until she pulled me away and screamed: "You don't kiss me like that!"

153

A few months before she came out, she walked into the den where I was watching TV and stood there, waiting until I looked at her. She was wearing a T-shirt and her breasts were loose, and she had the usual mysterious wet spot on the belly of her shirt from the ice cubes she chewed incessantly. She was a small woman, all torso, with a large round middle, and from the angle where I lay on the couch, her thighs looked like tiny triangles.

"Do you think you might be gay?" she asked me.

I was annoyed. It was the middle of the day and I was trying to watch TV. What had I done that was gay? I realize now that she was really asking me if I thought she was gay.

"No, I don't think so."

"Because you're very pretty, you know, and you could have some boyfriends. I've seen how boys look at you."

"Boys don't look at me," I said.

"Yes, they do."

We were quiet for a few minutes after this, so I turned the TV up. Another episode of the same show I'd been watching for hours came on, a sleepaway-camp comedy where boxers were raised up the flagpole in the opening credits.

"Doesn't it repulse you, the thought of two women or two men together?" she asked.

I turned the TV down again, but I didn't look at her. There was this one time, just as my breasts came in, when she had her arm around me on this same couch and started rubbing my breast. I froze and we watched TV like that for a while, until I finally asked her what she was doing and she pulled her hand away and said: "I thought it was your shoulder."

On the TV now a boy played a bugle as the shorts went up the flagpole, and I felt relieved that I found him cute.

154 "No, I don't think so."

"See, it repulses me," she said. "I asked your father and he said, yeah, it repulses him, too."

"I don't know what it looks like, so how can I say it's repulsive," I said.

"And you're sure you aren't gay?"

"I don't think regular sex is repulsive either."

"What do you know about regular sex?" she asked, her voice rising.

"From TV." And I turned it up again.

—

When my mom came out she acted timid at first. In a strange reversal, one day at the kitchen table I asked her if she was bisexual. It was after she told a long story about how she thought she might have been in love with a friend with whom she'd recently had a falling out.

She began to cry. "I don't know. Maybe."

A week later, as she drove me to a doctor's appointment, she had gained more courage.

"So it was that night when you and your father went to that baseball game, when I said I had the flu, that she first came into my bed."

I worried about what I might hear next. I pressed my body against the car door. I didn't think it was okay to ask her to stop, since she needed to tell someone, and she wasn't—I hoped—telling this to my father.

"That first night, we just held each other."

I could tell that she wanted me to ask her when they first kissed, or when something first really happened. But I didn't. I realized that my father would have asked these questions, and

155

I pictured him late at night on the couch, watching TV, knowing more than he needed to and still wanting to know more—specifically, the moment he lost her. All three of us were learning that he never really had her.

"I'm not lonely, kiddo," my father said late one night before the divorce. Worried about him, I had gone downstairs to join him in front of the TV. "How could I be lonely? I got you."

—

The next morning—my period steady but now painless—I asked my father if it would be okay if I hung out with a friend for the afternoon. Jess rented an apartment a few blocks away from where he lived, and she had suggested I come by and see some of the books she was reading for school. I felt guilty as I asked him. I was meant to spend my weekends with my dad, and I didn't know what he would do without me around. But how could I not hang out with Jess when it consumed every part of me, and when I wouldn't have to worry about my mom's prying?

My dad popped waffles out of the toaster, put one on each of our plates, and peeled an orange for us to share.

"That's fine. I have some errands to run that would be boring for you anyway. I have you for dinner tonight, though, right? Promise?"

"Maybe we can go see a movie, too," I said. I wanted him to feel that what I was doing was obligatory for my age, that I couldn't help it, that I didn't know any better than to hurt him in this very small way.

Jess's apartment was kind of like any other teenager's room, except she had a kitchen stocked with things like Oreos, ramen, spaghetti, and tuna fish. She had even made a pitcher of red

Kool-Aid and put out on the table a little bowl of crispy, spicy peas (wasabi, she told me later). The kitchen opened up to the living room, which had a yellow couch, a piano bench as a coffee table, some spider plants that crawled along the dusty edges of the floor, and a stereo playing Ravi Shankar. In her bedroom, which was painted a deep blue, there was a mattress on the floor, a full-length mirror, a set of plastic bins that must have held her clothes, a poster of a Black woman with an Afro, her eyes seemingly focused on something significant in the distance, the words "Free Angela and All Political Prisoners" over it. Jess had written underneath in large block letters: WHEN ONE COMMITS ONESELF TO THE STRUGGLE, IT MUST BE FOR A LIFETIME.

"What's the struggle?" I asked.

"For me, all of it. Angela Davis is referring to communism."

"Communism," I whispered, and I took a last look at the bedroom and thought I saw a haze within it, as if stepping into it could mean entering another world.

In the fall, Jess had taken a history class on liberation struggles and that was where she encountered Davis.

"It blew my mind, reading her and getting to see racism as this systemic problem, rather than just individual. That with the common racist," she tapped her hand on the piano bench, and I flinched, "it's a poisoning that comes from this small percentage of wealthy people—capitalists—who are making money off of racism, so it's like this plague that we've been tricked into and perpetuate. I mean, look at Asbury. All the money for this town went up some mayor's nose, and no one gave a shit about it. Then some gay white guys from the city decide to try their hand at business where the rent is cheap, and suddenly lots of really cool gay people from the city are coming here. Here. And all the nervous closeted Shore kids start hanging out and spending their money and getting laid and making it cool. Then other artists start coming in, then college students. Next thing my homophobic mom will go out for a night in downtown Asbury and the only thing that will have improved is the five-dollar coffee, not the conditions of the people. See what I mean? Isn't that amazing?"

I froze. I pictured the face of the man who had stepped aside, whose expression, I was certain then, blamed me. And I didn't want to be blamed. I wondered if Jess thought I was racist, then decided that she thought that I wasn't racist, which was why she was telling me this, but then realized that she would probably especially tell this to someone who was racist because that's part of the struggle. I chewed the wasabi peas very slowly and began to sweat.

"What do you like to read?" she asked.

My mind went blank. I scanned her bookshelf and spotted a name I knew.

"I read this Elizabeth Bishop poem in English class that I loved. I was helping another English teacher clean out her room after school one day and I saw a copy of that book and took it home. I've read some of her other poems too, but I mostly just keep reading that one about losing stuff."

Jess's face went soft again. I checked her hair, which was puffed up ... sensually, it seemed.

"'The art of losing isn't hard to master,'" she said.

"Yes!" I said.

"Oh damn, that ending," she said, closing her eyes. "'Though it may look like—'"

"'*Write* it!'" we both cried out at once.

Then her *Hoo! Hoo!* filled the air, and that was when I leaned over and kissed her cheek.

She was a teenager then, too, and I'll bet that Jess in her twenties, and especially thirties, wouldn't kiss back a sixteen-year-old who quoted Elizabeth Bishop to her. But eighteen-year-old Jess did kiss me back. My tongue stabbed wildly in her mouth at first, until hers asserted a kind of quality control. Eventually, I got the hint to mimic her, to slow down, to take her tongue in my mouth like I was taking all of her into my mouth. I say this now with the kind of insight that comes after throwing away everything.

We kissed as we moved down the hallway, and I pulled away enough to tell her that I had my period, because I had seen that in a movie on Cinemax. The woman told the man, and then he stuck his hand down her pants to check, and they didn't have sex. Jess didn't put her hand down my pants in this moment. She just kissed my neck and said huskily, "I don't care." And then, "But feel free to use the bathroom if that would make you more comfortable."

As I peed, I felt dizzy with the sense that my life was happening, the same kind of thrill of that first month of my period but much more intense. My pubic hair was sticky with blood, and I cleaned myself with toilet paper. This was the first time I had experienced my own slickness. I had to touch myself gently because I was swollen and it appeared that the whole apparatus could just cave in or tear. I found a fresh pad under the sink and affixed it to my underwear. This didn't make me feel sexy, but I didn't quite know what else to do.

While we undressed each other, I glanced at the poster and wondered if the eyes were watching us, like the Mona Lisa, but these eyes stared intently at something else—the revolution—beyond us. As Jess kissed down my thigh, my body tensed and

159

I thought again how at some point even a revolutionary leader feels something like this, even the common racist.

"You cold?" she asked.

I nodded. She removed the rest of her clothes—her bush was not big like the woman in the seventies book from the store, was in fact a bit more kept than mine—left on my giant diaper, and rested her body on top of me. This was meant to warm me, as a kind of interlude, but I groaned as soon as we made contact in this purposeful way, and she groaned and locked her arms around me and we were moving.

I felt her pubic bone, then flesh, against my thigh and something mysterious, like the energetic expression of desire, and when she pressed against me it was really as if she pressed into me.

"What are we feeling?" I asked.

She pulled my underwear down and I met her thigh.

We started off rocking like this, and though it would seem so disappointing if it were filmed—so hetero, so chaste—it didn't feel like any of those things.

"Can you come?" she asked.

She gently pressed her hand against my throat—she was introducing me to something else I wanted.

"Come, now."

So I did. I thought of my mom as I came, her hand on my breast. I shook my head and my orgasm was interrupted. I felt Jess continuing to come on top of me.

We rested. The light changed to that odd blue, too light for headlights, too dim to see. Through the walls were the sounds of the other tenants making dinner. I dozed. Maybe I could move into this room and quote poems and eat wasabi peas and do this

160

with Jess underneath the eyes of the revolutionary and learn how to not be to blame.

Then I remembered my dad and I pulled myself up. Jess suggested I wash my face before heading home, and tie my hair into a bun so that my dad wouldn't smell her when he hugged me. When I walked away from her apartment the streets looked wider and whatever chill was in the air stung the raw skin around my chin. *If she knows whether she loves someone after the first time she has sex, shouldn't she have told me she loved me right then?* I hadn't asked her how that worked and now I was missing a crucial piece of information. I was gripped by a new kind of fear that seemed more devastating than anything I had experienced before: that I could love someone and not be loved in return.

The next morning I told my dad that I couldn't spend the day with him, that I had to study at a friend's house, and this time I was filled with such urgency that I didn't even feel guilty for leaving him alone. In fact, I resented him for his loneliness, for the fact that he loved someone who didn't love him back, and I didn't want that disease to live in me, to ever live in me.

—

I didn't tell my mom about Jess, not because I didn't know what to talk about, but because I decided not to talk to her at all.

"Is something going on," she asked one night, standing imposingly in the doorway of my room. "Are you dating someone?"

"No. Don't ask me that," I said firmly, violently.

She looked stunned. Her breasts swayed as she turned, and she didn't ask me again until the next night during dinner.

"Someone named Jess called for you," she said, watching me for a reaction.

I gave her none. I chewed the tough meat on my plate until I couldn't anymore, and then spit it into my napkin. I took a bite of mashed potatoes with a spoonful of peas. My mouth was too full to speak.

"Honey, is this someone that you're, I don't know, dating?"

"Mom. No."

"Because I found this book under your bed, with these images—you don't need to hide it. You don't need to hide who you are. I don't think I need to tell you that you can date who-ever you want."

A buzzing rage vibrated over my head, and I pushed away from the table.

"I'm not like you. The thought of it—it repulses me."

My mom picked up her glass and she looked ready to throw it at my head, but instead, she slammed it down on the table and let out a sob, a sound so terrible and long, one that I didn't want in my ears, so I let it rush through me and tried not to feel it. Something inside me that the moan should have penetrated stepped aside and never quite stepped back.

—

The next day, after school, I saw Jess. In class that day, she told me, they'd done an exercise where they had to get in pairs and say a cultural group—Chinese, Indian, African American, Mexican, Caucasian—and state all the stereotypes that came into their heads.

"It was so hard. I was forced to look at what was inside of me, and it was awful," she said. "There were a few white students who left the room, and I wish I could be like, 'You aren't a bad person, but you have to look at this. It needs to burn so we can see more clearly.'"

We were naked and I had my head nuzzled under her chin and I held on to her tighter. I stared at the poster: WHEN ONE COMMITS ONESELF TO THE STRUGGLE, IT MUST BE FOR A LIFETIME. I was determined to tell her that I loved her. I was going to tell her. I opened my mouth to say it, finally, when she removed herself from my arms.

"You're holding me a little too tightly," she said, and patted my hand.

I turned away from her and allowed my hurt and discontent to fill the room.

"Darlin,'" she said.

I loved when she called me that, but I wasn't ready to respond. There was something I was noticing. She'd recently acquired a night table where we'd taken to burning a candle while we were together. It had burned down to the very base of the holder, and I became so transfixed by the flame that the sob left me.

Suddenly, it wasn't a candle anymore; it was just a flame, and it looked so tired leaning its weight against the edge of the base. It leaned like it knew it was about to end. I was too young—no, too privileged—to truly know about things and their endings, how suddenly they come, but I felt it in that flame. I grabbed another candle from the drawer, because it felt important to me, I cannot explain why, that I use that flame to light another candle. And for a few brief moments, the flame existed in two places, on my new candle and the dying one.

"Do you have scissors?" I asked.

She kissed my shoulder, then got up. I heard her rummaging around. I wanted to tell her to hurry, but I didn't yet know I could make demands of someone that I loved who might not love me back. She handed them to me and I used the scissors to gently nudge at the side of the wax, removing the still-lit disc,

163

which balanced on the blade of the scissors as I inserted the new candle. The new flame seemed silly and young. It was this dying flame that I loved. I thought that it might make it for a time. This flame was the strongest thing I'd ever seen.

Chinese, I thought to myself and waited: a laundromat, a plate of dumplings, a cartoon drawing of a face—I don't know where I'd even seen it, which is to say I'd always seen it. I didn't want these images, and I heaved them off, felt them dissolve into that empty place that my mother's sob passed through the night before. I watched the wick fall over and go out.

"No, no," I said. I pressed my hands onto my chest. "No, no." Jess put her hand on my thigh, but I couldn't feel it. "I don't want to see that."

"What? The candle?" she said.

"I'm not ready."

"It's not about being ready."

"I wasn't ready."

"But it's good. We got this new candle now, and it's brighter." She kissed each eye; she kissed my lips. "You just hadn't noticed the other one until the end. That's okay, because now you'll pay more attention to this candle. We can watch it burn together."

She held my hands too tightly and I looked at her lips and I could see that there was more that she wanted to say and now I didn't want it, I didn't want another word, or for Angela Davis to look at me in that cluttered, Nag Champa–scented room. I felt the edges of cramps coming on, like a white hand with long pink nails squeezing my uterus and pulling down. I asked Jess to drive me home.

"Can I walk you to the door?" she asked when we were outside my house.

I was in so much pain, I barely shook my head. I didn't want my mom to see her. I could never tell her about Jess. I didn't want to see the disgusting delight in her eyes, or the dimming in my dad's. I didn't even look at Jess to say goodbye. Somehow, I found myself standing at my front door, my hand shaking as I unlocked it.

That night, as I writhed on the floor, waiting for the whisky to take effect, I decided that I wouldn't see Jess anymore.

It was so easy to let go.

There are certain rules you learn early.

ACKNOWLEDGMENTS

I thank Wendy, Ann, Rae, and Melissa for the support, strategies, and medication that has kept me here and full of desire to see this moment (and all that's to come).

For deep reading, critique, and friendship towards this manuscript and me, I thank: Mattilda Bernstein Sycamore, Anca Szilágyi, Nancy Jooyoun Kim, Michael Heald, Lacey Jane Clemmons, Jennifer Natalya Fink, Michael Heald, Paul Lisicky, Rebecca Brown, and Melissa Febos.

I thank Brian Lam for bulldozing the wall and taking this book on—and so many writers at Arsenal whose work in print helped me to imagine this one there, too. Thank you to Shirarose Wilensky for encouraging me to probe deeper to find something new and dazzling in these stories, to Jazmin Welch for the gorgeous design, and to Cynara Geissler and Mandy Medley for brilliantly getting this book into readers' hands—a profound task, all.

Thank you to Amanda Kirkhuff for a perfect painting.

Since this is my first published book, I offer gratitude to various mentors throughout my life: Kat Grausso, KT Langton, Peter Trachtenberg, Vijay Seshadri, Rachel Cohen, Joan Silber, Rebecca Lee, Karen Bender, Monica Lewis, Nicole McCarthy, and especially, Betsy Teter.

Thank you to Artist Trust for funding and time to work on these stories at Centrum Artist Residency. Thank you to the

MacDowell Colony and to the brilliant residents there that August and September 2015 when the initial manuscript was completed—a special nod to Ian Miles Gerson and Jeremy O. Harris for cracking the blood-filled egg.

Thank you to the Hub City Writers Project.

Thank you to Theresa and Jackie, Talia, Bekah, and Sydney, Cara and Ben, Courtney, Eli, Frances, Bunny, Anis, Chelsey, Nicole, and Emmett. To my students, Hugo House, Seattle Arts & Lectures, and the sprawling and inspiring Seattle writing community.

I thank the Mannings née Manzellas, the Giustis, the Gallos, and the Natellis.

My biggest thanks to Erin Sroka, Roderick McClain, Ever Jones, and Harlan Fern McClain: the chambers of my heart.

Shannon Perez-Darby and Daniel Hanson, thank you for helping me change the narrative of how it is possible to love and be loved.

Finally, thank you to everyone I've ever loved/made out with since spring 2004. You are not in this book and yet:

All my life,
since I was ten,
I've been waiting
to be in
this hell here
with you;
all I've ever
wanted, and
still do.
—Alice Notley

To all other writers and readers: MWAH!

Photo Credit: Itzel Santiago Pastrana

CORINNE MANNING is a prose writer and literary organizer whose stories and essays have been published widely, including in *Toward an Ethics of Activism* and *A Shadow Map: An Anthology by Survivors of Sexual Assault*. They have received grants and fellowships from the MacDowell Colony, Artist Trust, 4Culture, and the Hub City Writers Project. Corinne founded the *James Franco Review*, a project that sought to address implicit bias in the publishing industry.

corinnemanning.com